To the Saline Library

Stetbyd

Second Wind Publishing

Look for more coming soon from

Steve Hagood

www.secondwindpublishing.com

Chasing the Woodstock Baby

By

Steve Hagood

Cut Above Books
Published by Second Wind Publishing, LLC.
Kernersville

Cut Above Books
Second Wind Publishing, LLC
931-B South Main Street, Box 145
Kernersville, NC 27284

First Cut Above Books edition published
January 2015.
Cut Above Books, Running Angel, and all production design are trademarks of Second Wind Publishing, used under license.

For information regarding bulk purchases of this book, digital purchase and special discounts, please contact the publisher at
www.secondwindpublishing.com

Cover design by Stacy Castanedo

Manufactured in the United States of America
ISBN 978-1-63066-100-7

For Jenni. Thanks for always believing.

PROLOGUE

1969

Caroline and Randy stood on the sidewalk next to the VW microbus. The VW was loaded and ready to go. Caroline could tell Randy was stoned. Not that that was unusual, he was usually stoned. His blond hair, thinning already at the ripe old age of 20, shot out from his head like a sunburst. He wore a pale yellow "Keep on Truckin'" tee shirt, cut-off jeans, and sandals.

"Come on, Caroline," Randy said, "it'll be fun."

"Look at me," Caroline said, running her hands over her swollen belly. "I'm pregnant. Very pregnant."

Randy pouted like an eight-year-old. "You're not due for another month at least. It will be fine."

Caroline sighed. She looked over Randy's shoulder at the driver of the VW. He was small and wiry. He wore no shirt with his cutoff jeans. Long, greasy, scraggly hair hung loose to his shoulders. Thick sideburns peeked out from behind the hair. His eyes were hidden behind mirrored aviator glasses.

"I don't even know these people," she said.

Randy looked quickly over his shoulder and then back. "That's Steve. He was in my American Lit class last semester."

"You didn't take American Lit last semester."

"I didn't?" Randy searched his memory, confusion clouded his face. "Well, that's Steve," he said. "Steve is a good guy. He'll take care of us."

"I don't know," Caroline said. "How did you hear about this again?"

"Steve told me about it. Come on Caroline. Joan Baez is supposed to be there. You like her."

Caroline did like Joan Baez. But she was eight months pregnant and Bethel, New York was at least a ten hour drive. She really didn't want to go, but Randy was looking at her with those eyes. She had never been able to resist those eyes.

"Oh, what the hell," she said. "Let's go."

Randy whooped and they climbed aboard the VW headed for the Woodstock Music & Art Fair.

When Randy had said New York, Caroline had pictured skyscrapers and bright lights. She was looking out the window at pastures and farms and open spaces when Steve pulled the microbus to the side of the road.

"Is this it?" Randy said. He craned his head in all directions, looking frantically. "I don't see anything."

"Not sure," Steve said, "but everybody seems to be parking here on the side of the road. I guess this is it."

Caroline was ready to get out of the VW. It had been a long drive, and she was not feeling well. She and Randy climbed out, along with Steve and the other girl who had ridden with them. They all strapped on backpacks and started walking. None of them knew exactly where they were going, but they joined in with the crowd. Someone up ahead must've known the way.

Caroline had never seen anything like it. Cars parked bumper-to-bumper lined the road as far she could see. Thousands of people walked in the same direction, intent on getting to where they were going. It was hot, and after about 15 minutes of walking, with no end in sight, Caroline was really beginning to feel bad.

Randy took Caroline's pack, and helped her as she struggled up the road. Steve and the other girl never broke stride, and began to disappear from sight. Caroline saw swimming pools in the back yards of a few of the houses along the road. She would love to have stripped off her clothes and taken a dip, along with some of the other hippies who were partaking. She assumed they had not been invited to swim, but that sure wasn't stopping them.

Finally, after what seemed like hours of walking, they crested a hill and saw before them a sea of people. It was amazing. Caroline had no idea how many people there were. Randy led her along the edge of the crowd. A wooded area ran up the side of the open field. He found a small patch of ground that provided some shade, dropped their packs, and proclaimed that they had arrived.

Caroline eased down onto the grass, propped her head on her backpack and tried to relax. The concert had not yet started. She dosed fitfully while they waited.

Richie Havens had just been announced when the first real labor pain hit. Caroline screamed. A few people nearby took notice, but none did anything to help. Randy held a pill in front of her eyes and told her to take it.

"It will help with the pain," he said.

Caroline had gone cold turkey when she had realized that she was pregnant. Well, mostly. She had definitely stayed away from any hard drugs, but had occasionally joined in when a joint had been passed around. She did not want to take the pill that Randy offered, but when the second labor pain hit she agreed. She washed it down with a swig from the canteen Randy held in front of her. Within minutes she spun off into a psychedelic world free from pain.

CHAPTER ONE

August in Detroit. To say that it was hot would not do justice the misery that hung over the city. The above normal temperatures and humidity that had Detroit in its grips was entering its third week, and not giving any indication that it would relent anytime soon. It was the sort of heat that makes the citizens of the city that Forbes Magazine ranked the most miserable city in America crazy.

I had already heard stories of people snapping in the heat. A man honked his horn when the pickup truck in front of him at a stoplight was too slow, in his estimation, to go when the light turned green. The driver of the truck took his tire iron to his impatient fellow motorist's windshield. A woman beat her toddler half to death when the poor kid spilled his milk. At least she hadn't cried over it. Another man shot his wife when dinner wasn't on the table when he got home from work at the factory. The fact that she was in bed with the flu apparently didn't matter.

I had retired from the Detroit Police Department earlier in the year. I had pursued a suspect in a case, against direct orders from an assistant chief. The suspect had been a city councilmember's son. There is a lot a Detroit cop can get away with, but going after a councilmember, or a councilmember's family is not one of them, especially if the councilmember has an assistant chief in her pocket. They would have fired me outright if they had thought they could get away with it. Unfortunately for them, the kid had been guilty, so they took the prudent path and allowed me to retire early. I hadn't wanted to retire, but it'd been the best deal I was going to get. So, whether I liked it or not, I was no longer a cop.

I had been given the opportunity to buy into O'Ryan's Pub and took it. I was partnered once again with my old training officer, Sarge. I wasn't out sweating my ass off on a hot August afternoon amid the crazies. All in all, things could've been worse, I guess.

It was quiet in the bar. I was trying to match invoices to packing lists, and struggling. Apparently fifteen years as a cop does not prepare one to run a business. Who knew? Sarge was behind the bar, working a crossword puzzle.

Nicholas O'Ryan had been a first-generation American whose parents had come over from Ireland. He hadn't intended for O'Ryan's to be a cop bar, but it was close to the station and the cops adopted it, way before my time. Nick had run the bar until the day he died, literally. He had dropped dead of a heart attack while tending bar. A portrait of him hung behind the bar, flanked by photos of Nick with 50 years of police chiefs, from George Edwards to James Barron.

Sarge retired soon after Nick's death, and bought the bar from his estate. The proceeds from the sale went to the Detroit Police Officer's Association. The cops had been the only family Nick had had. Sarge had retired with full honors, a full pension, and a badge in a Lucite block. A picture of him with the current police chief hung near the Nick O'Ryan shrine. The only thing I had as a souvenir of my career was the chief's boot print on my ass.

"What's a five letter word for pursue?" Sarge asked.

"Really?" I said.

Sarge looked at me, perplexed. "What?"

"Chase."

"Oh, right," he chuckled. "I was just messing with you." He dropped his head to enter the letters into the boxes.

The bar door opened and a lady walked in on a ray of sunshine. We got non-cops from time to time. They were usually people from out of town in for a Tigers game or a concert. But I didn't remember many single women darkening our door, especially one like this.

She was tall and thin with long arms, made longer by the sleeveless, yellow top that she wore with a flowing, flower print skirt. Her hair was cut very short and gray. She reminded me of my third grade teacher, Mrs. Fanning, except for the gray hair. She stood by the door for a moment, letting her eyes adjust to the darkened room, and then walked to the bar.

Sarge ran a beefy hand across his thinning white hair and sucked in his gut. "Well, hello," he said. "What can I do for you?"

"I'm looking for a man named Chase," the lady said, somehow controlling herself in spite of Sarge's smooth hair and sucked in gut.

Sarge let out his gut and hooked a thumb at me like a hitchhiker. The lady looked down the bar to where I sat. I tipped my beer bottle at her in greeting.

"You're Chase?"

"You found me," I said. "And who might you be?"

She stared at me a moment, and then shook herself out of whatever she was thinking. "I'm sorry. My name is Caroline Wolf. I looked for you at the police station, but they said you had retired, and suggested I look here."

"And here I am," I said with my warmest smile.

"Yes, I suppose you are," Caroline Wolf said.

She stood and stared at me for a moment. She didn't seem too happy with what she had found. It was giving me a complex.

I took a drink from my bottle. "Was there something you needed?"

"I need your help."

I led Mrs. Wolf to a booth against the far wall. It wasn't that I wanted to get away from Sarge, but I could tell that this nice old lady had something serious to talk about, and I didn't want her to have to unload whatever it was, standing in the middle of a bar. I slid in across from her and waited.

"My daughter is sick," she said. The light that hung above the table reflected off gray eyes that sparkled like silver. "She has aplastic anemia."

I had no idea what aplastic anemia was, or what it had to do with me, but I sat quietly and listened. Something Mrs.

Fanning had taught me.

"It's a condition where the body stops producing new blood cells," Caroline Wolf continued. "The doctors think a bone marrow transplant is her only hope, but we need to find a donor. Sara, my daughter, has a rare blood type. They think a sibling would be her best hope for a match." She paused for a beat, again leading me to wonder what this had to do with me. "I have another child, but I don't know where."

"This child is missing?" I asked.

"I'm sure that this child is right where it belongs, I just don't know where that is."

That didn't make any sense, and I noticed she called the child "it" and not he or she. "Wait a minute," I said. "You're telling me your child is not missing, but you don't know where…it is?"

"That's right."

"You lost track of it?"

"Sort of."

I felt as if I was trying to help Sarge find his car keys. "Where did you last see it?" I asked, feeling like an idiot.

"Woodstock."

"And..." I started to say, and then realized what she had said. "Did you say Woodstock?"

"Yes."

"*The* Woodstock?"

"Yes."

"Three days of peace and love, and all that?"

"Yes."

I thought I must have heard wrong. "The Woodstock Baby," I said. "You're telling me you gave birth to The Woodstock Baby?"

"I am," Caroline Wolf said, nodding her head. "Will you help me find it?"

CHAPTER TWO

"By the time I came down from whatever it was that Randy had given me, Joan Baez was just going on. She was the last act of the first day. Whatever Randy had given me had taken the whole day from me. I wasn't really concerned about the concert, I was more concerned about my baby."

I had been transfixed by Caroline Wolf's story. I had heard the legend of The Woodstock Baby—supposedly amid the half-million people in attendance at the festival a baby had been born. However, 43 years had passed since the concert and nobody had ever come forward and claimed to have given birth to it, or actually to be it. I, like most rational people, had equated The Woodstock Baby with Bigfoot, Area 51, and the JFK assassination conspiracy. But here I was, sitting across the table from a 60 something-year-old, recently retired third-grade schoolteacher—yes, Caroline Wolf had been a third-grade schoolteacher just like Mrs. Fanning—who claimed to have indeed given birth to The Woodstock Baby.

"So what happened to the baby?" I asked

Caroline Wolf stared off into space. Tears filled her eyes. "Randy told me it was dead. He said it had been stillborn, and that he had buried it off in the woods."

"And you believed him? He carried a baby into the trees in front of all those people and buried it?"

"I know. Looking back now it doesn't make sense, maybe it never did. I don't know. I was pretty messed up at the time, and if I'm truly honest with myself, maybe I wanted it to be true. I was nineteen years old and in no position to be a mother. So maybe I believed Randy, because I wanted to."

"I'm not judging you," I said. I don't know why, but I felt like I needed to say it.

"Yes, you are," Caroline Wolf said, looking me dead in

8

the eyes. The tears had evaporated. "And that's okay. I'm not proud of it, Mr. Chase, but it happened. It is what it is. When we got back to school I broke it off with Randy, stopped taking drugs, and started concentrating on my studies. My family never even knew that I had been pregnant, and I never told anybody my story before today. I would've taken this to the grave, if Sara hadn't gotten sick."

It was a difficult story to believe, but somehow I believed her. This nice old lady seemed rational and very believable, and she had bared her soul to me. "Why do you think the baby is alive?"

"It has to be," she said. "If that baby is dead, then so is Sara."

"Why me? Why did you come to me?"

"I read about you in the paper; about how you refused to back off that city councilmember's kid. My daughter's life is on the line. I need someone who won't back off, no matter what."

I thought about it for just a second. The truth of the matter was that running a bar was boring me to death, and I wasn't very good at it. I missed the action being a cop provided, and drinking every night with my old friends and listening to their stories could only take me so far. So, I told Caroline Wolf I would do what I could to help her find her baby. It was then that I realized that the baby was not a baby anymore but was actually my age. If I wasn't sure that my mother was my mother and that I'd been born in a hospital in Detroit, I could've been The Woodstock Baby. I showed Mrs. Wolf to the door, and then sat back at the bar.

"You believe her?" Sarge said.

"Sure," I said. "Why would she lie about this?"

"It could be a publicity stunt," Sarge said. "Maybe she thinks she can find a donor for her daughter."

"You're right, Sarge. But look around. Where are the TV cameras? If she wanted publicity she would've told her story to TMZ, or Katie Couric, or something like that."

"The kid is probably dead."

"Maybe," I said. "But we have to find out for sure. If that kid is still alive, and can save the life of the other kid, then I have to try."

"Why you?"

I felt a surge of adrenaline enter my veins. For the first time in months, I felt as if my life had purpose. I smiled, "If not me, who?"

CHAPTER THREE

I had never been much of a researcher. Back when I was on the force I usually let my partners do the research. I also had a connection at one of the newspapers in town, a reporter named Trudy DeRosa. Trudy and I had spent five or six years using each other for information, and sex when neither of us was seeing anybody else. I met Trudy for breakfast the next day at the American Coney Island in downtown Detroit.

American Coney is a true landmark in Detroit. It sits on a peninsula of land where Lafayette and Michigan Avenue come together. It has been in business and owned by the same family since 1917. For a business almost a hundred years old, it is very clean. The floors are black and white checkerboard. The tables and chairs are all chrome and red vinyl. Windows on both the Lafayette and Michigan Ave. sides of the restaurant let in a lot of light.

I was sitting at a table by the windows on the Lafayette Street side when Trudy entered. She took my breath away, literally. She wore in a low cut, very tight white top that showed most of her cleavage, and a short black skirt that showed most of her legs. Her black hair was cut in a kind of chopped Joan Jett style that was sexy as hell.

She strode to the table on four-inch heels, while every man in the restaurant watched. She grabbed a fistful of my shirt, just below the collar, and pulled me up from the chair. She planted a kiss on my mouth that curled my toes, and then pushed me back down into the chair. "Hello, Chase," she said.

I took a moment to catch my breath, while Trudy slid onto the chair across from me. "Hi Trudy," I managed to say.

Trudy leered at me. I knew she was just messing around, but it was fun nonetheless. "Long time," she said. "Where you been?"

"Retired," I said.

"What's that got to do with anything?"

I was saved when the waitress brought coffee. I ordered eggs, bacon and hash browns. Trudy ordered toast.

"So what did you come up with?" I said when the waitress had left.

Trudy smiled at me. "Business before pleasure, huh?"

She confirmed what I already knew. No one had ever come forward and claimed to have given birth at Woodstock, or to have been born at Woodstock. The local clerk's office had not issued any birth certificates that weekend either.

There were a few people who claimed to have been part of a birth at Woodstock. A man named Elliot Tiber, who director Ang Lee featured in his film "Taking Woodstock," claimed to have helped deliver a baby the weekend of the festival at his parent's motel near the concert site. He said he never got names, and never heard from the people again. He couldn't have had anything to do with the delivery of Caroline Wolf's baby anyway because she said she had given birth on the festival grounds, not at a motel.

The concert's medical director, a man named Abruzzi, reportedly told interviewers that there had been two births at the concert. But, when he wrote up his official report, he chronicled six pages of incidents, including 707 drug overdoses, but he didn't mention anything about the two births. Had he simply forgotten them? Or had he been convinced to exclude the births from his record? I was pretty sure that I would never find out because Dr. Abruzzi was dead.

The waitress had brought our meal, and I had scarfed mine down while Trudy had reported.

"So what's this all about?" she said.

"Just looking for some information," I said.

"Is there a story in this?" Trudy asked, in full reporter mode.

"If all goes well," I said.

"I'd better get the exclusive."

"Of course. I owe you."

"That's not all you owe me," Trudy said, leering again.

CHAPTER FOUR

After my "retirement" I had purchased a black Dodge Charger from a Sheriff's Department auction. The former patrol car was stripped of all evidence that it had once been a patrol car, except for the engine and handling package. It was beat to hell, but it fit me and I loved everything about it. I climbed into the Charger, full of bacon and eggs, and happily indebted to Trudy DeRosa. I couldn't wait to pay her back.

Randy Adams had left Eastern Michigan University shortly after returning from Woodstock. Was it because Caroline Wolf had dumped him? Was it because his child had died? I figured I'd just ask him. Caroline had told me that Adams had returned to his hometown, which was only about 40 miles west of Detroit.

I took I-94 out of the city. The landscape grew more and more rural the further I went. I felt like Dorothy in the Wizard of Oz traveling from a world of gray, to one of color. The grass that I could see was green and dotted with various colors of flowers. The sky even seemed bluer once I got outside Detroit city limits. I exited the highway at the Saline exit.

I was a bit taken aback when, after following the cloverleaf from under the overpass to the top, I found a four-lane road with not much traffic. Sure it was the middle of the day and most people were at work, but I wasn't used to driving on such deserted roads. I followed Michigan Avenue further west. I passed a gas station, a trailer park, more gas stations, a Sam's Club, passed over another highway, and continued on until I passed a Walmart on the outskirts of Randy Adams' hometown. Traffic picked up as I approach the downtown area, and I found a bustling city.

Saline appeared to be just like every other small city you hear about. There were a couple restaurants, a couple bars, a couple banks, a bakery, two barbershops, and several small niche shops. What I didn't see were bars on the windows, burned out husks of buildings, homeless people panhandling on the streets, or hookers hanging out on the corners.

I cruised the streets for a while, getting a feel for the city. The houses were all well-kept with manicured lawns. Kids played in the backyards, road bikes on the sidewalks, and sold lemonade from stands. I found the police station a block off of Michigan Avenue. It shared a building with the City Hall. It was mostly brick with green tinted windows. The entrance didn't face the street but the parking lot, which seemed weird.

I parked in the lot with several other cars, including two white police cruisers. I stepped out of the car and into the suffocating, wet blanket humidity. I wondered why they had used so much green as I pulled open the heavy green entrance door.

I entered the building and allowed the cool, air-conditioned air to wash over me. It had been no more than 20 steps from the car to where I stood, but I had already started to sweat. I stood just inside the door, taking in the high-end surroundings. It was quite impressive, right down to the city seal inlaid in the floor.

A door opened to my left and a giant of a man walked through. He hooked his thumbs in his wide leather gun belt and eyed me. He was easily 6'4" with a physique that Tigers analyst Rod Allen would've called "country strong." Arms like sides of beef protruded from the short sleeves of the dark blue uniform shirt. His brown hair was cut blunt and plain; it looked as if a sheep shearer had done it. The name tag on his uniform said Ford. He reminded me of an F-250.

A large smile, full of large white teeth lit up the big man's face. "Good morning," he said. "I'm Officer Ford. What can we do for you today?"

"I'm looking for a man," I said. "I hope he still lives here."

"This a friendly visit," Ford said. The light in his face faded, replaced by a look of concern.

"Yes. I'm just looking for some information, and I hear he can help me."

"Looking for information? Who are you?"

"I'm sorry," I said, offering my hand. "My name is Chase."

My hand disappeared into Ford's giant paw. "Glad to meet you, Mr. Chase. But that doesn't tell me who you are."

"I'm just a guy, looking for a guy."

Ford looked skeptical, but said, "So who is this you're looking for?"

"His name is Randy Adams. He should be in his early 60s."

Ford took his head slowly, thinking. "I don't believe I know him."

"You're sure?"

"Randy Adams is dead."

Ford and I both turned to the voice. It came from a short, wiry guy who looked immaculate in the same navy blue uniform that Ford wore. His hair was silver and slicked back, and his face was tanned. His nameplate said Hannigan.

"Chief?" Ford said.

"What do you mean dead?" I said.

"As in no longer alive," Hannigan said.

"When?"

"About 35 years ago."

That's not good, I thought. "How?"

"He was hit by a car."

"An accident?"

Hannigan nodded. "Yes. Randy was high, as usual, and walked out in front of a car."

"Is the driver still in town?"

"He's dead."

"What?"

"Killed himself."

I shook my head in confusion. "Wait a minute," I said. "You're telling me the guy I'm looking for, and the person who killed him are both dead?"

The chief's eyes narrowed. "What are you implying?"

"I'm not implying anything," I said, returning Hannigan's scowl. "I'm simply stating facts. And those are the facts as you know them?"

"Yes. Those are the facts as I know them."

CHAPTER FIVE

I left the police station not quite sure what to do next. It hadn't gone anywhere near how I had expected. First and foremost, I hadn't expected Randy Adams to be dead. I don't know why I didn't expect it. He was supposedly in his sixties. Many people didn't live that long, especially if they had drug problems to the extent that Randy Adams seemed to have had. Buty I still hadn't expected it. The hostility from Chief Hannigan had also been unexpected. Why had he gotten so worked up about my questions? Was it just because I was questioning his police force? Or was there something deeper there?

I got back in the Charger and fired it up. I left the police station and realized I didn't have a plan B. That might have been a good time to come up with one. I recalled seeing a shopping center, with a couple small restaurants in it, on the way into town. It hadn't been that long since breakfast, but what the hell, I could eat again.

I sat in a vinyl booth under a mural of a 1950s theater. An Elvis Presley movie was advertised on the marquee. What would Elvis have done? Probably sing a song. Too bad I can't sing. A young, blonde waitress took my order and returned about seven minutes later with a cheeseburger and fries that actually looked halfway decent.

"You wouldn't happen to know anything about a man named Randy Adams, would you?" I asked as she slid the plate in front of me.

The girl cocked her hip and rested her hand on it. She looked like the little teapot. "Did he go to Saline?" she said, thinking.

"I'm pretty sure he did," I said, encouraged. "Graduated around 65 or 66."

"*Nineteen* 65?"

Embarrassment replaced the encouragement. "Yes."

She laughed. "Dude. My parents aren't even that old."

"Oh, right," I said. Her parents were probably my age. "Thanks anyways."

"No prob," she said with a smile. I watched her walk away. She wore those black yoga pants that all the kids are wearing these days. I always feel like a pervert when I look at a young girl wearing them.

"Excuse me."

I turned to the lady in the booth across the aisle from me, thinking I had been busted. She might have been attractive, if I could have gotten past her hair. It was black and cut in sort of a bob, I think. It was real short up the back of her head and then got longer as it moved forward toward her face. From the side it looked like the Atlanta Falcons logo.

"I couldn't help but overhear."

"No prob," I said, mimicking the young waitress, relieved that I hadn't been exposed as a pervert.

"You said you're looking for Randy Adams?"

"Well, I'm looking for information about Randy Adams. From what I hear, he died about 35 years ago."

"I don't know anything about him," the lady said, "but I work over at the EVH, the evangelical home, and there is a resident there named Agnes Adams. She's always going on about her son Randy."

"Really?"

"Yes, but she talks about him as if he's still alive. Of course no one has ever seen him. She had a stroke a few years back and her memory is kind of scattered. Maybe he's the Randy Adams you're looking for?"

"Where's this home?" I asked, feeling as if I might have stumbled onto plan B.

CHAPTER SIX

My new friend's name was Misti, "with an i." She was in her early 30s, I learned while we ate our lunch, and was divorced with three kids whose no-good father never saw them, and didn't give a damn about them.

"I mean I love those kids and all, but it would be nice to get a break now and then, you know? Why can't he take them once in a while?"

I shrugged my shoulders and pretended to listen while she told me all about it, because she had promised to take me to the evangelical home and introduce me to Mrs. Adams. We finished our lunch and I offered to buy hers in exchange for the favor she was going to do for me. I didn't have to twist her arm very far. Misti drove a minivan that had seen better days, but started right up and sounded just fine. She wore blue track pants with a white stripe down the side and a polo shirt with the EVH logo on the breast. She also wore a brand-new pair of Nike running shoes. I wondered how much of her no-good ex-husband's child support had been used to pay for them.

Misti led me back through the downtown area and took a right at the American Legion. Two blocks up there was a blue sign with a white H on it and a white arrow that pointed to the left. I took that as an indication that the hospital was that way. Sure enough, Misti turned left and we entered a small hospital complex. I knew, from Misti's having told me, that the hospital was outpatient only. She didn't have much hope for it to stay open much longer. The evangelical home was a wing of the hospital, with a separate entrance. We parked and entered through a set of double doors akin to an airlock. I was immediately hit with the smell of every old folks home I never been in, a combination of cleaning agents, misery, and looming death. I wanted to leave before we were three steps inside.

Misti said hi to everybody we passed, like a homecoming queen waving from a parade float, which she had told me over lunch that she had been. We entered a very blue open space that served as the reception area. The walls were painted blue, the carpet was blue, and the furniture was all different shades of blue. Misti pointed to a little blue-haired old lady, sitting in one of the chairs. I thought at first that the blue hair was somehow caused by all the blue that surrounded her, but then realized she actually had blue hair. I had always thought the blue-haired old lady thing was just a figure of speech, because I had never actually seen a blue-haired old lady, but Mrs. Adams certainly had blue hair. She also had skin so thin and pale I could see her veins, like one of those visible man models they had in the Our Body exhibit at the Detroit Science Center. The veins and the hair actually complimented each other.

"That's her," Misti said and walked towards her. "Remember what I told you about her."

Remember what she told me about her? She hadn't said a word about Mrs. Adams during lunch. She had talked about herself the entire time.

"Hello, Mrs. Adams," Misti said, leaning over with her hands on her thighs, speaking to the old lady as she would a child.

"Hello," Mrs. Adams said, as if she had never laid eyes on Misti before. I was a little bothered by her tone. I had paid for Misti's lunch because she said she knew Mrs. Adams.

Misti was un-deterred. "How are you today?"

"Have we met?"

I looked at Misti. Her cheeks had reddened. "I'm Misti. I work here."

"She doesn't know you, you ditz," a gravelly voice said.

I looked over to another old lady, sitting nearby in a wheelchair, obviously eavesdropping on the conversation. She had hair the color of dirty snow on the side of the road,

21

styled in a comb-over, and not doing a very good job of covering the top of her head. She wore what looked like a shower curtain for a dress, and the legs that stuck out of the bottom looked like cement pillars.

Misti turned to her. "Please, Mrs. Norman," she said. "What have we told you about your language?"

"Screw you," Mrs. Norman said. "You treat us like children around here. I'm an adult for crying out loud."

"I know you," Mrs. Adams said, but she was talking to me, not Misti.

"You do?" I said.

"Yes, you live down the road from us, in that green house next to the woods."

I didn't know what to say. I must have reminded her of an old neighbor.

"If you came to see the baby, she's not here yet."

"The baby?"

"My granddaughter. Randy said he was going to bring her for a visit, but they haven't arrived yet."

I started to speak but Misti grabbed my arm. She leaned in and whispered in my ear, "This is what I was telling you about. Her memory is all over the place. Although this is a new one, I haven't heard anything about a granddaughter before."

"What's your granddaughter's name?" I asked Mrs. Adams.

"I don't know," Mrs. Adams said. "Randy just said it was a girl, and he would bring her by for a visit. I'm so excited. Randy is my only child you know, and I just can't wait to get my hands on that baby."

"Randy's dead," Mrs. Norman said.

"Mrs. Norman," Misti hissed.

"And there ain't no granddaughter."

"Mrs. Norman--"

"She sits there all damn day, waiting for her dead son to bring his imaginary child for a visit."

I tried a different approach. "Does Randy have any friends in town?" I asked Mrs. Adams.

Mrs. Adams thought a minute. "Most of the kids he went to high school with are off to college," she said.

Mrs. Norman scoffed. I shot her a look and she backed off.

Mrs. Adams continued. "But I see the Hannigan boy around a lot--"

"The police chief?" I said.

"What? No, Michael Hannigan."

"Remember," Kelly said softly behind me.

"Oh, right," I said to Mrs. Adams, "my mistake. Anybody else?"

"Randy used to pal around with Rick Leland, but they had some kind of falling out. I'm not sure what it was over, but I see Rick around town every now and then."

"Thank you, Mrs. Adams," I said. I said goodbye to Mrs. Norman and left.

Misti walked me back to the door and punched in the code to unlock it. I thanked her for her help, and as I left the building I felt her shove something into the back pocket of my jeans. I pulled the piece of paper out of the pocket as I walked to my car and unfolded it. The note said "call me" and was signed Misti, with hearts dotting both of the i's. A phone number was written underneath.

A patrol car was parked behind my car, blocking it in. Officer Ford was leaning his ass against the rear fender of the patrol car. His arms were folded across his chest, his right ankle was crossed over his left, and a cheesy grin was on his face.

"You're a cop," he said.

I crumpled the note from Misti, and deposited it in a trash can as I passed it. "What makes you say that?" I said.

"I was curious, so I Googled you."

"You Googled me? You don't strike me as the Googling type."

"Yeah?" Ford said. "What type do I strike me as?"

"I don't know," I said. "The tractor pull type?"

Ford laughed. "I do that too."

"Well I'm not a cop anymore," I said. "I own a bar now."

Ford pressed on as if he hadn't heard me. "What you said earlier, about the guy you're looking for and the guy that killed him both being dead."

"What about it?"

"I did some digging. The kid who hit Adams was named Peter Wilson. He was 18 at the time. Less than a year later, he stepped out in front of a dump truck and was run down and killed."

"Seems a little coincidental, doesn't it?" I said.

"It does. So what are we going to do about it?"

"We? I'm not here to dig into a 30-year-old suicide."

"What are you doing here?" Ford said, nodding his head at the hospital

I looked back over my shoulder. "I was visiting Randy Adams's mom."

"Why? You said you were looking for him. He's dead. Why haven't you left town?"

"Well, the truth is I was looking for Randy to help me find someone else."

"That's going to be tough with him dead," Ford said.

"It is," I agreed.

CHAPTER SEVEN

I found Rick Leland right where Ford said he'd be, in a 20' x 40' pole barn on a dirt road about 15 minutes south of town. An American flag waved proudly at the top of a tall pole with an eagle perched on top. A POW/MIA flag waved just below it. The grass was mowed crisp and clean and the trees were well on their way to maturity. It looked like he had been there a while, but I didn't see a house.

Leland had gray hair pulled back into a ponytail, with a mustache of the same color drooping over his upper lip. He wore cut-off jeans and a tank top. The skin that covered his long, lanky frame was tanned and leathery.

He let me into the pole barn, explaining that after he had bought the property he couldn't get it to pass a perc test, and the township wouldn't let him build a house. After he explained that a perc test has to do with ground water and a septic field – I grew up in the city, there is no reason for me to know any of this stuff – he said they did allow him to build a pole barn. So he did, and moved into it, without water. Somewhere along the line they finally found a way for the land to pass the perc test, and he was finally able to get water. But by that time, he was comfortable in the pole barn, so we stayed. Though he did run the water into it.

The pole barn was set up loft-like. The kitchen, living area, and bed were visible from the door. Only the bathroom, which was added later, was enclosed. I actually thought it was pretty cool. Because of the flags outside, I had expected the inside to be decorated Soldier of Fortune style, but I was wrong. The decor was all earth tones.

"You want a beer?" Leyland said, pulling two cans of Pabst Blue Ribbon from the refrigerator.

"No, I'm good," I said.

He shrugged and put one of the cans back. "So what can I do for you, Mr. Chase," he said, popping the tab on the beer and straddling a stool that sat beside the island counter that separated the kitchen from the living room.

"I hear you were friends with Randy Adams back in the day."

"Randy Adams," Leyland echoed in the soft voice that he spoke with. "I haven't heard that name in more than 30 years."

"You knew him?"

"Sure. In high school."

"How about after high school?"

"After high school I went to Vietnam, by way of Paris Island."

"Marine, huh?"

A small smile formed under the droopy mustache, and he took a pull from the beer. "Semper Fi," he said.

"Randy didn't go to Vietnam," I said.

"No sir, he did not."

"How did he stay out of the war, and you didn't?"

Leland took another pull from the Pabst. "I ran into Randy at a little get together one night not long after I got back. I asked him that same question."

"And what was his answer?"

Leland took a quick breath in through his nose and held for a second. He finally let the breath out and said, "He said he had something The Captain wanted."

"The Captain?" I said. "What Captain?"

Leland smiled his little droopy mustache smile. "You're not from around here," he said as if he hadn't realized it before.

"No," I admitted. "I'm not from around here. What Captain?"

"*The* Captain."

"The police chief?"

Leland shook his head. "The police chief's daddy. He was the chairman of the local draft board. He decided who got drafted, and who didn't. He used that power to build his little empire."

"What empire is that?"

Leland chuckled and swung his arm in an all-encompassing motion. "This one. He owns pretty much the whole damn town."

"And Randy had something The Captain wanted, and used it to buy his way out of being drafted."

"That's what he said."

"What was it?"

Leland shrugged his bony shoulders.

"Come on," I said.

"Randy didn't say."

"You didn't ask?"

"It didn't matter."

"Did you kill him?"

"Did I kill Randy?"

"Randy's mom said you had a falling out. Was it because you got drafted and he didn't?"

Leland shrugged those bony shoulders again and finished his beer. "Mister," he said, setting the Pabst can on the counter, "I did two tours in 'Nam and printed books at the printer here in town for the next 30 years. Was I mad when I got drafted? Sure. Did I resent Randy for not getting drafted? Sure. But I got over it, and Randy was dead before I could make amends. And no, I didn't kill him."

CHAPTER EIGHT

I left Rick Leland's house and headed back to The D. There was more I probably could have done in Saline, like check out this Captain, but I have to admit I was anxious to pay back Trudy. It'd been a while since Trudy and I had been together. Memories of some pretty wild and crazy nights flashed before my eyes as I drove.

I stopped by O'Ryan's to check in on Sarge. As I entered the bar I saw a stunningly beautiful woman sitting on my regular barstool, sifting through my papers.

"Uh, hello," I said.

She looked up at me. Her green eyes sparkled. "Hello," she said.

"What are you doing?" I said, pointing at the papers on the bar.

"My uncle asked me to help out."

"Your uncle? Who's your uncle?"

She pointed behind me. I turned to see Sarge coming through the swinging door that led to the back room.

"Is he in the back room, talking the Sarge?"

"Only if he was talking to himself."

I love Sarge like a father, but there is no way this lovely creature was from the same gene pool as Sarge. "Sarge?" I said in disbelief.

She nodded.

"You're Sarge's niece?"

"You're quick," she said with a giggle.

"I'm sorry," I said, looking back and forth between her radiant beauty and Sarge's Easter Island head. "I just can't believe that you and Sarge are related."

"I'm Sally," she said, offering her hand.

"Chase," I said, taking her hand in mine. It was small and smooth and cool.

"Aha, the infamous Chase."

I bowed, and then couldn't believe I had done it.

Sally laughed. "Very smooth."

I shook my head. "Sarge! Give me a beer!"

I slid onto the stool next to Sally and Sarge brought me a beer.

"How's the case going?" Sarge asked.

I told him about the trip to Saline, and the conversations with the cops and the others.

Sarge's eyebrows rose. "You think the thing that Adams had that Hannigan wanted was the baby?"

"I don't know. Could be."

"But didn't Caroline Wolf say that she rode back from Woodstock with Adams?"

"Yes."

"Without the baby?"

"Yes."

"So what happened to it?"

I took a long pull from the beer bottle, and then set it down and wiped my mouth. "That's the question, isn't it?"

CHAPTER NINE

I drove back to Saline the next morning, thinking about Sally the whole way. We had spent most of the evening sitting at the bar, talking and getting to know one another. She was light and airy, absolutely refreshing to be around. Because of my career and location, I had spent the majority of my adult years in a dark, depressing place. Sally was a ray of sunshine unlike any I have ever seen before.

I hadn't thought at all about The Woodstock Baby, but I refocused as I drove. I was intrigued by Leland's statement about Adams having something that Captain Hannigan wanted. It was too much of a leap at this point to suggest it was the baby, and I couldn't go accusing him until I had proof. And I had no idea how I would get proof, if it even existed.

I cruised past the Walmart and the car dealerships on the outskirts of town. I saw red and blue flashing lights in my rearview mirror as soon as I passed the sign that indicated that I had entered the city limits. Like all normal people my reaction was to look at my speedometer to see how fast I was going, and then look for the speed limit signs around me. I quickly determined that I wasn't speeding, and had no idea why I was being pulled over. I eased to the side of the road in front of an enormous factory, and slammed the car in the park. I looked in the side mirror. The police cruiser pulled to a stop behind me and an enormous cop climbed out of the driver's side door.

"Son of a bitch," I muttered and put the window down.

Ford's walk reminded me of that famous Bigfoot video.

"Morning, Mr. Chase," he said

"Officer Ford," I said. "Is there a problem?"

"I need your help with something."

"What's that?"

"I've been going over the case files in the deaths of Randy Adams and Peter Wilson."

I groaned.

"Hear me out," Ford said.

I sighed. "I'm all ears."

"Okay," Ford said, adjusting his gun belt and preparing himself as if he was auditioning, and this was his make or break moment. "Peter Wilson told the responding officers that Adams came out of nowhere. He had been under the influence of drugs, and they wrote it up as a simple accident. Drugged up guy walked out in the middle of the road and gets hit by a car. Case closed."

"And?"

"Something doesn't feel right about that."

"It was more than 30 years ago, Ford," I said. "Why are you bringing this to me anyway? Why not go to your detectives, or the chief, with your suspicions?"

Ford fidgeted uneasily. "Okay, look," he said, "there's more going on here then you realize."

"There'd have to be."

"I don't think the whole accident story, or the suicide story for that matter, are on the up and up. Everybody in this town knows that The Captain can, and will, do whatever he wants, to get whatever he wants."

"So you have an axe to grind with The Captain," I said.

"No, that's not it. The Captain has this whole damn town under his thumb. It's time someone stood up to him, and took the town back."

"And that someone is you?"

"Sure," Ford said, fidgeting, "why not?"

"Why not indeed?" I said.

"But I need your help."

"Why?"

"Because I don't know what the hell I'm doing."

CHAPTER TEN

"What the hell," I said. I didn't believe it was any more than a really sad coincidence, but Ford was a good guy and I liked him, so I decided to go along. "Lead on, Officer."

Ford spun on his heel and literally ran back to his patrol car. He jumped in and laid rubber taking off. I'm not sure how he didn't hit me. I followed in his wake. He hadn't turned off the flashing lights on the roof and traffic parted in front of us. We pulled to the curb in front of a small ranch house with white, chalky aluminum siding and faded black shutters, across the street from an elementary school, in a quiet neighborhood. Ford jumped out of his car.

I climbed from my car and said, "Do we really need the lights?"

Ford looked as if he hadn't realized they were still on. "Oh, I guess not," he said, and reached into the car and shut them off.

"Okay," I said, "who are we seeing here?"

"Peter Wilson's parents, Warren and Evelyn."

"Both are still alive?"

"Yes, believe it or not. They're both in their late seventies. I talked to Mrs. Wilson earlier, and she said they would be happy to talk with us."

"So they know we're coming, huh?" I said. I tried to convey with my voice, and the look on my face, that I knew he had planned on my accompanying him the whole time.

"Yeah, well, I figured you'd want to be in on this."

"In on what? There's nothing to be in on."

"Let's just go talk to the Wilson's, and see what we think afterwards."

I waved my hand in an after-you gesture. Ford hustled in front of me, up a concrete walk that split the lawn. His wide leather gun belt squeaked with every step.

His knock was answered by an average looking seventy-something-year-old lady with white hair and reading glasses, hanging on a gold chain around her neck. Her hair looked as if she had just come from the beauty parlor, and the makeup she wore was so minimal that you had to really look to pick up the red of her lips and cheeks. She smiled but the smile didn't reach her eyes. I had seen it many times before. There was real loss in her eyes. I had never had children, let alone lost one, so I didn't judge the fact that she looked as if she was still mourning the loss of her son after forty years. A tall beanpole of a man with a big mop of white hair loomed over her shoulder. He was freshly shaven and wore a Hawaiian shirt and baggy shorts.

"Mrs. Wilson?" Ford said. "I'm Officer Ford. We talked this morning on the phone?"

"I remember, Officer," Mrs. Wilson said. "Won't you come in?"

"Thank you ma'am," Ford said, following the old couple into their home. He introduced me when we reach the living room.

"Are you a police officer too?" Mrs. Wilson asked.

"No."

Ford jumped in. "He's retired from the Detroit police."

"Detroit?" Mr. Wilson said. "You're a little out of your jurisdiction, aren't ya?"

"Yes sir, I am," I said. "I'm in town on an unrelated matter, and agreed to accompany Officer Ford here today. Is that okay? I can wait outside if you'd rather."

"No-no, sit down?" he said, pointing to a couch covered with a wild, flower pattern. "No sense in you sitting out there in that heat." It wasn't much cooler in the house than it was outside.

Ford and I sat. The couch was as comfortable as it looked, which was not at all, but I wasn't planning on staying long.

Mrs. Wilson offered us drinks which we both declined. Then she sat in a chair that matched the pattern of the couch. Mr. Wilson stood behind her, ever looming.

"We're here to ask you some questions about your son, Peter," Ford said.

"Okay," Mrs. Wilson said. She glanced at a framed 8 x 10 picture of a skinny kid in a blue suit with hair parted on the side and black horn-rimmed glasses. It looked like my, and every other kid's, senior picture from high school, except for the styles.

We all looked at the photo for a moment as Ford tried to come up with a question to ask.

"Tell us about the accident, when Peter was driving," he finally said. "When he hit Randy Adams."

"That damn hippie," Mr. Wilson muttered.

"Warren," Mrs. Wilson said.

"Warren nothing," he said. "That kid was always stumbling around town, high on one thing or another. Everybody knew it. It was only a matter of time before he got hit by a car."

I looked at Ford with an I-told-you-so look.

"He didn't deserve to die, Warren," Mrs. Wilson said.

Ford returned to look.

"Oh, I guess not," Wilson said, "but it destroyed Peter, and he didn't deserve that."

"Folks," I said, getting their attention. "Can we start at the beginning?"

"Peter was on his way to pick up his girlfriend Jenny, and go to a movie. We weren't worried about him. He was a good driver."

"Taught him myself," Mr. Wilson said. His voice was filled with pride, but also a challenge for us to dispute the fact that he had taught his son to be a good driver.

"He hadn't made it to Jenny's house yet, when Adams popped out from between two cars, right into his path," Mrs. Wilson continued. "He couldn't stop, there was no time."

"Excuse me, Ma'am," Ford said, "but Peter told the responding officers that he didn't know where Adams had come from."

"Yes, at first," Mrs. Adams said. "He was terribly shaken after the accident."

"So when did he decide that Adams had 'popped out from between two cars'?" I said.

Mr. Wilson glared at me.

"You have to understand," Mrs. Wilson said, "Peter was very young, and having killed a man, even if it was an accident, was too much for him to handle. He was despondent and withdrew from life. We ended up taking him to a psychiatrist, hoping he could help him learn to deal with it."

"And?"

"Peter was making progress. I think he realized that it wasn't his fault and was learning to forgive himself. Little by little the old Peter was coming back."

"But he killed himself," I said.

"No!" Mr. Wilson said.

"The report said he intentionally stepped out in front of that truck," Ford said.

"He did not," Mr. Wilson said. His voice conveyed that his mind would not be changed on the subject.

"They had a witness."

Mr. Wilson scoffed. "Witness," he said.

"Warren," Mrs. Wilson said.

Mr. Wilson waved a hand at his wife in a dismissive way.

"You don't believe the witness?" I said.

"I wouldn't believe Charlie Johnson if he told me my name was Warren Wilson. I would have checked my driver's license, to be sure."

I laughed, in spite of the situation. "Is Charlie Johnson still in town?"

"Charlie died some years back," Mrs. Wilson said. "Lung cancer."

"Did Charlie have sons?" I asked.

"What's that have to do with anything?" Mr. Wilson said.

"Yes, Charlie had two sons," Mrs. Wilson said. "Terry and Cliff."

"Did either go to Vietnam?

She thought for a minute. "I don't think so. Terry went to college."

"And Cliff?"

"I don't think he went to college," she said, shaking her head.

"And didn't go to Vietnam? Did he join the National Guard?"

"I really don't know," Mrs. Wilson said, shaking her head.

CHAPTER ELEVEN

Ford pretty much skipped down the sidewalk as we left the Wilson's house. He stopped when we reached the road and smiled at me. "I told you there was more to the story."

"You did," I admitted. "So now what?"

"I don't know. What would you do?"

"Well, you have to find someone to corroborate the Wilson's story. Who do you think could do that?"

Ford thought for a second. "Maybe we can track down the old police chief."

"He probably wouldn't corroborate the story," I said, "since he's the one who probably covered it up, if there was a cover-up."

Ford thought for a second. "If there was a cover-up, how would you prove it?"

"How about the girlfriend?" I said. "Maybe she can tell you some things that his parents don't know. Teenagers usually don't tell their parents everything."

"Is she still around, and even alive?"

"Why are you asking me? How the hell would I know?"

"Oh, right," Ford said. "I guess I'll go see if I can find her."

"Good idea," I said. "In the meantime, I'm going to see what I can find out about The Captain and his draft board."

"What was that all about anyway?"

The sun had reached directly overhead, and the day was really starting to heat up. Sweat was starting to drip down my ribcage.

"What was what about?" I said.

"All that stuff about Charlie Johnson's sons, and did they go to Vietnam?"

"I don't know," I said, shrugging my shoulders. "Just seemed relevant."

"Bullshit," Ford said. "What do you know that I don't?"

I could think of a long list of things that I knew that Ford probably didn't know. I tried to read him. Could I trust him? I had ideas in my head that could be dangerous in a small town, especially one controlled by a single man.

"How about your dad?" I said. "Did he go to Vietnam?"

"Nah," Ford said, shaking his head. "He was too young for Nam."

Ford's dad probably was not that much older than I was, I realized. Damn I was getting old.

"What do you know about The Captain?"

Ford shrugged. "I don't know, just what everybody else knows, I guess. He owns just about everything around here."

"So The Captain runs the town?"

"His kids pretty much run the place now," Ford said. "His son is the police chief, his daughter is the mayor, and another of his kids owns a bar. But what does The Captain have to do with Randy Adams and Peter Wilson?"

"I don't know. All I know is Charlie Johnson witnessed Peter's suicide and his sons didn't get drafted. Coincidence?"

Ford started to talk and I cut him off.

"And, Randy Adams told someone that he didn't get drafted because he had something The Captain wanted. And then he ended up dead. Coincidence?"

"You really think it's not a coincidence?"

"I don't know at this point." My cell phone rang in my pocket. I pulled it out and check the caller ID. "Go find the girlfriend," I told Ford as I flipped open my phone.

"What girlfriend?" Caroline Wolf said in my ear.

I climbed into the Charger and started it up to get the air conditioner going. I watched Ford drive away. "It's nothing," I said into the phone. "It's an unrelated topic."

"Oh, okay," she said. I could hear confusion in her voice, wondering why I was working on something other than finding her baby. "I was just calling to check in. Are you making any progress?"

"Randy Adams is dead," I said.

"Oh no, that's too bad," she said.

I didn't know if she meant it was too bad he was dead, or too bad that he couldn't help us. I told her about meeting Randy's mom.

"I met her once," Caroline Wolf said. "Randy brought me home to go to a party. One of his high school friends was going off to Vietnam. We stopped by and saw his mom before going to the party. She seemed like a nice lady."

"Did you meet any of his friends?"

"I met a lot of people. I think his whole graduating class was there."

"Did anyone stand out to you?"

"Stand out? What do you mean?"

"I don't know. I'm just trying to find out who's who here. I found a friend of Randy's who told me that he, Randy, told him he stayed out of Vietnam because he had something The Captain wanted."

"Who's The Captain?"

"The man who runs this town. He was the head of the local draft board, and it sounds like he extorted bribes in exchange for deferments."

"Did Randy give him my child?" Caroline Wolf asked.

"I don't know," I admitted. "What else would Randy have had to trade?"

There was a long pause, and then in a quiet voice she said, "Nothing."

CHAPTER TWELVE

I found the public library next to the middle school. The school was huge, and had its own football stadium, baseball field, and tennis courts. The parking lot was almost empty, as would be expected in the middle of the summer. The library was cool and sort of quiet. There were a lot of teenagers hanging out. I didn't see any of them reading. They were sitting in groups talking and flirting. I guessed there were worse places they could have hung out. None of them paid any attention to me as I walked past.

As I said, I've never been much of a researcher. So, I walked to the reference desk, and asked the bored looking librarian at the desk where I could find information about the city, and Captain Hannigan in particular.

Her hair was in a bun and she wore glasses way down on the tip of her nose, and a denim jumper over a long sleeved turtle neck. She couldn't have looked more like a librarian if she had tried. Her eyes, already larger than normal because of the thick lenses of her glasses, grew even larger when I mentioned The Captain.

"Is there a problem?" I said.

"No," she said, trying very hard to sell it. "I could set you up with some microfiche films from the Saline Reporter, but they won't tell you very much about The Captain. He keeps a pretty low profile."

"Well then, where can I find information about him?"

The librarian looked around furtively to make sure nobody was listening, and then said in a hushed voice, "Art Pindar."

"Who's Art Pindar?"

"He used to own the local paper. Now, he's our town historian."

I looked around furtively, to amuse myself. "Where can I find him?"

"He's usually over at the Train Depot Museum."

I got directions to the Train Depot Museum and thanked librarian for the information. I then left the library and walked to my car. The air had changed while I had been inside. The sky had darkened and it smelled as if a storm was brewing. I was eager to find out what a train depot museum was. Apparently, somebody didn't want me to see the train depot museum because before I could pull the Charger door open, someone smashed me in the back of the head with something that felt like a battleship.

CHAPTER THIRTEEN

I came to on an old wooden floor, staring at a dirty ceiling. A single dim light bulb hung directly overhead, attached to a wire. They hadn't given me a pillow, let alone a bed or cot. I tried to sit up and the world spun. I laid back down and waited for the ride to come to a complete stop. As I lay there I tried to remember how I had gotten there, and why my head hurt so damn much. It wasn't the first time I ever woke up on the floor with a headache, but those times usually followed a night of fun. And then it came to me. I remembered briefly being hit on the back of the head and I had a very brief recollection of being shoved face first into my car.

My brain wasn't working very well, but I soon realized I was probably in danger. I rolled onto my stomach and walked my feet towards my head, trying to stand up without actually lifting my head off the floor. Eventually I had to lift my head. I used the ripping-the-Band-Aid-off technique and straightened to my full height all at once. Bad idea. The world started to spin again, and I staggered in a looping circle trying to balance my head above my shoulders.

I had almost got it, and then someone pushed me. I staggered to my left and crashed into a tower of boxes, falling in a heap among them. Someone laughed.

A raspy voice said, "Knock it off. Get him out of there."

Two strong hands encircled my ankles and I was pulled unceremoniously across the wood floor. I squeezed my eyes shut against the spinning.

"Open your eyes," the raspy voice said.

I did as instructed and found myself looking into the droopy, watery eyes of an old man. He had parchment like skin, shaved smooth, wild snow white eyebrows, and more liver spots on his head than hair.

"I hear you've been asking all over town about me," he said.

"I don't even know who you are, you crazy old man," I said.

Another bad idea. A foot crashed into my ribs. It wasn't from the old man, he hadn't moved.

"Son of a bitch," I said with what breath I could muster. "What the hell was that?"

The old man, who I figured was The Captain, pointed a gnarled finger in my face. "I don't like people asking questions about me. Fuckin' stop it!"

And then the foot that had assaulted my ribs crashed into my head and the world went black again.

The next time I came to, I was strapped into the driver seat of my car. The storm that had threatened earlier had come, and sheets of rain hit the windshield as if I was in the middle of a car wash. From what I could see I was on the side of the road, just outside the city limits, pointed east toward home. It was nice of them to have put me in the seatbelt, but I had a crick in my neck from my head lolling to the side. They had left me a note. Don't come back was written across the windshield with a black magic marker.

I wasn't about to run from this guy, especially if a life could be saved, but I figured they had someone waiting to pull me over and resume the beating were I to cross back into town, and I was in no condition to protect, or defend myself. I started the ignition slammed the car into drive and headed back to Detroit.

CHAPTER FOURTEEN

I sat at the bar in O'Ryan's and chased a handful of aspirin with a cold beer. Then I filled Sarge in on the case.

"So what's your next move?" Sarge said.

"I'd like to find this Steve Belloti. The guy who drove them to Woodstock."

"You think he knows anything?"

"I don't know," I said. "But it can't hurt to ask."

I worked on my beer while Sarge brought me up to date on the bar. Nothing exciting had happened while I was gone, except that Sally was starting to make some headway with the paperwork. According to Sarge the heat was helping business. Our former colleagues were hiding out in the air-conditioning and drinking. It was way better than spending their down time mowing the grass and washing the car, especially in the heat.

Sally came from the back room waving a piece of paper. She grinned from ear to ear and was so excited she bounced. "Steve Belloti is a lawyer in Southfield," she said. "He specializes in labor law."

"What?" I said.

"Belloti and Associates in Southfield," Sally said, shoving the paper into my hand. "Graduated from Eastern Michigan in 1970 and U of M law in '73."

"What's labor law?" Sarge said.

"He represents employees in disputes with management," Sally said.

"Where did you get this?" I said, scanning the paper.

"There's this thing called the Internet," Sally said as if she was talking to a four-year-old.

"You mean that thing Al Gore invented?"

"Yeah that's it. You ever been on it?"

"I don't have a computer."

"There's one in the back room."

44

"You mean that thing Sarge plays solitaire on?"

"Yeah, that thing," Sally said. "You're being facetious, aren't you?"

"Yes, I am. I know about the Internet, and how to use it. I just choose not to."

"So I shouldn't look for you on Facebook?"

CHAPTER FIFTEEN

I woke the next morning in a bit of a daze. It took a while before I could remember the events of the previous day. Apparently whoever had hit me, and then kicked me in the head had done more damage than I had originally thought. I remembered eventually, and it pissed me off. I remembered looking into the rheumy eyes of the old man as he tried to run me off. I realized that his threats had the same effect on me as the councilwoman's threats. I was more determined than ever to see this thing through. I guessed Caroline Wolf had been right about me.

My first stop of the day was Southfield. It wasn't exactly on the way to Saline, but it was where Steve Belloti was, and he was first on my to-do list.

I took the Lodge freeway north out of the city to where it dumped into "the mixing bowl." The mixing bowl was where a confluence of highways came together – M-10, I-696 and US-24 specifically.

As the exodus of people and businesses had left Detroit over the last forty years, Southfield had become the business center that Detroit had once been. It's signature landmark being a cluster of office towers known as The Golden Triangle. Officially named The Southfield Town Center, the five golden, interconnected skyscrapers housed more than two million square feet of office space, as well as a hotel, restaurants, and a conference center. More than 100 of the Fortune 500 companies have offices in Southfield. While Detroit sat decaying a mere fifteen miles south, Southfield thrived.

Steve Belloti's office was not in The Golden Triangle, but in The American Center building. The stand-alone 26 floor high rise was impressive in its own right with more than 600,000 square feet of office space.

I entered and took the elevator to the tenth floor where Belloti's office was located. Just under halfway up, the tenth floor was not one of the "power floors", but it wasn't bad for a one lawyer law firm.

After a forty minute wait I finally made it past the receptionist and entered Belloti's inner office. It only took a minute to see the reason he had selected this building to house his office: it had an outstanding view of the Reuther Freeway (I-696). It probably didn't mean anything to anybody else in the building, but for Belloti, a labor lawyer, looking out over the highway named for the trailblazing UAW president Walter P. Reuther, it probably meant everything. It was a daily reminder of his lot in life and the footsteps he was trying to follow in.

He greeted me with a smile and a handshake. His pudgy hand was sweaty in mine. His suit coat hung on a hook on the back of the door, but the tie was still high and tight, squeezing his many chins up. They threatened to spill over the collar of a white shirt that struggled to contain a gut constructed over several decades by tens of thousands of beers.

Belloti offered me a chair and circled a desk that sat perpendicular to the view, always keeping the late Mr. Reuther in sight. The air rushing through his nose sounded like a locomotive and I couldn't imagine how hard his heart was working to keep him alive. He didn't come close to the image I had in my head of the rail thin, scraggly haired hippie that Caroline Wolf had described.

"So, Mr. Chase," he said, consulting a yellow legal pad that sat on the desk in front of him. "How can I help you?" His voice sounded as if he gargled with asbestos every morning. His gregarious personality filled the room. This was a man who had had The Big 3 over a barrel more than once. I could understand where that would give a man a certain confidence, but I was about to take it all away. My head still hurt and I was pissed about being left sitting in the outer office for almost an hour, so fuck him.

"I need some information from you," I said.

Belloti looked confused. His eyes darted quickly to the door behind which his secretary sat, to the legal pad where he had started to take notes, and back to me. "You need information? From me? I don't understand. I thought you were here on a legal matter?"

"I am," I said. "I just need your help to determine whether it's accomplice to kidnapping or accomplice to murder that I tell the DA to charge you with."

It was my favorite technique. Screw the carrot, go right for the stick.

Belloti's eyes darted wildly around the room as if he was looking for hidden cameras or something. "Wait a minute," he said. "What the hell is going on here? I don't know anything about kidnapping or murder. Who the hell are you anyway?"

I ignored his question. "You went to Woodstock, right?"

Now he was really confused. "What?"

"Don't try to deny it. I have witnesses. You drove a white VW microbus with an assortment of tie-died peace signs painted all over it."

"Deny it? Why would I deny it?"

"You drove there with a guy named Randy and his pregnant girlfriend."

"Yeah, so?"

"You returned with Randy and his no longer pregnant girlfriend, but not the baby."

Belloti paused with his mouth open, and then said, "Oh shit," softly. Beads of sweat popped out on his forehead, and rings formed in the underarm regions of his shirt.

"Exactly," I said. I leaned over the desk, trying my damndest to bore my eyes through the back of his skull. "What happened to the baby?"

"I don't know. I swear."

I let him simmer for a long moment and then turned away. As I walked to the door, I said, "Who was the girl that went with you?"

"The a—"

"The girl," I snapped, spinning back toward him. "What was her name?"

"It was…um…Judy. Judy Wilde."

"Where can I find Judy Wilde?"

"I don't know," Belloti said, "I swear. I haven't seen her in thirty years."

"I better not find out you lied to me," I said, and then marched out of the office like the prick I had just acted like.

CHAPTER SIXTEEN

It took the better part of an hour to get from Southfield to Saline. In that time the handful of aspirin I had taken finally started to get the upper hand in the battle that was going on in my head, and I started to feel halfway human again. Art Pindar had agreed to meet me at a coffee shop just outside the city limits, across the street from the Walmart. I wasn't afraid to go back to The Captain's town, I knew eventually we'd have a showdown, but it wasn't the time for it. I couldn't let my desire to take the old bastard down get in the way of finding The Woodstock Baby. That was way more important than my wounded ego.

Pindar was waiting for me when I arrived. A cup of something covered in a mountain of whipped cream sat on the table in front of him. The table was small and covered in a mosaic of tiny blue tiles. Pindar was an elegant looking older gentleman. His white hair was perfectly cut and combed. He wore glasses with black horn rims on top and no frame on the bottom. His necktie and blazer were a little over-the-top for a coffee shop, especially on another 90 degree summer day, but somehow it worked for him.

"Thanks for agreeing to see me," I said. I pulled up a chair across from him and sat down.

"You're welcome," Pindar said. His small, yet elegant voice was a perfect fit for the small, elegant man. "You mentioned on the phone that you're looking for information going back quite some time."

I nodded and decided not to beat around the bush. "I'm wondering about the Vietnam draft. I talked to someone who implied that The Captain extorted bribes in exchange for deferments."

"Telling stories about The Captain can be dangerous," Pindar said, but didn't look scared.

"I'm aware of that," I said, smiling and rubbing the back of my head. "I don't want to put you in danger, and I wouldn't if it was an extremely important."

"Extremely?"

I nodded. "Life-and-death."

Pindar looked over the tops of his glasses at me. "Why don't you tell me what this is all about?"

I picked up a glass of water that sat in front of me on the table and took a drink while I thought. Thus far I had played it pretty close to the chest, not revealing my real mission to anybody in town. Eventually, I was going to have to trust somebody. I set the water glass down on the table and told him who I was looking for and what I had learned.

Pindar listened to my story without interruption. When I finished he took a second to process everything and then nodded his head. "I can confirm, but can't prove, that The Captain took bribes in exchange for deferments, but I wouldn't exactly call them bribes. He knew exactly what he wanted. When a young man's number came up, The Captain would approach the kid's family and demand what he wanted. He was very good at painting a picture of the war in Vietnam and insinuating that their little boy probably wouldn't come home alive."

"And people believed him?"

"He didn't have to work that hard. The war was on TV every night."

"Not everybody that went to Vietnam died."

"Do you have children Mr. Chase?"

"No."

"Then you wouldn't understand. There's nothing that a parent wouldn't give to save their child. Was it a stretch to believe their boy would die in Vietnam? Maybe, but for a terrified parent any chance was too much. The Captain accumulated percentages of businesses and farms. He took cash from those who had cash to give. A few families even gave him the deed to their homes. The Captain would allow them to stay in the homes, but they paid him rent at an exorbitant rate."

"Randy Adams told my witness that he stayed out of Vietnam because he had something The Captain wanted. You know what that was?"

"No," Pindar admitted. "I don't even remember the Adams family. They must not have been one of the more prominent families. Families that didn't have anything usually saw their sons go off to war."

"Is it possible that Randy Adams could have given a baby to The Captain?"

"I don't see how," Pindar said, shaking his head. "Mrs. Hannigan was very well known in town. Each of her pregnancies was common knowledge."

"Was one born in 1969?"

"Yes, the youngest, Meredith. She's the Mayor now."

"You know that right off the top of your head?"

"Absolutely," Pindar said, nodding his head. "There was actually a bit of drama involved. Mrs. Hannigan was past forty when she got pregnant. I can't begin to tell you how or why, but it was a very high risk pregnancy and Meredith was a very sick little girl when she was born. She was very small and very frail. She was kept in an incubator for quite a while. They didn't know if she would make it. A priest was called in twice to administer last rites. But she made it. Everybody in town knew about The Hannigan Baby in 1969."

"You wouldn't happen to know anybody who could tell me more about the ordeal?"

"Well, the family I'm sure."

I laughed and rubbed the back of my head again. "Besides the family?"

Pindar smiled. "Yes, of course, you don't want to ask the family." He thought for a minute and then said, "You know, I think Carol Stockton was working at the hospital around then."

"She was a nurse?"

"Yes."

"In the maternity ward?"

"I don't know that," Pindar said, "but if it had to do with The Hannigan Baby, everybody in the hospital would've known all the details."

CHAPTER SEVENTEEN

I left the coffee shop and stepped into the heat of the day. The previous day's storm had done nothing to ease the heat wave. If anything, it was hotter and steamier than it had been before. Tendrils of heat rose up off the black asphalt. I found Officer Ford leaning his ass against the trunk of my Charger. His big arms were folded across his chest, straining the short sleeves of his uniform. He had an I-know-something-you-don't-know smirk on his face.

"You selling tickets?" I asked.

The smirk left Ford's face. Now I knew something he didn't know. "Tickets? Tickets for what?"

"The gun show," I said, pointing at his arms.

Ford smiled. "Nope. No tickets. This is a private showing just for you." He flexed without uncrossing his arms, stretching the material of his shirt even further.

I chuckled. "What's up?"

"I found one of Charlie Johnson's sons," Ford said, releasing the flex of his arms.

"Good for you," I said. I looked up at the sun. "Sure is hot out here."

"You know," Ford said, "I'm supposed to report to the chief if I see you."

"Really? He put out a BOLO on me?"

"No, nothing official. He just wants to know if you're in town."

"You going to tell him?"

"You gonna come with me to talk to the kid?"

"The kid? He's probably in his sixties."

"You know what I mean. Will you do it?"

I really didn't want to. I wanted to find Carol Stockton. "I tell you what," I said, "I'll go with you to talk to Charlie Johnson's kid if you help me find Carol Stockton."

"Who's Carol Stockton?"

"You help me find her and I just might tell you."

Ford thought for a second. "Okay," he said. "Let's do it."

I rode with Ford in his squad car to a subdivision in the northwest corner of the city. We found Cliff Johnson sitting in a lawn chair just inside his garage, watching two huge chocolate labs sniffing around the perimeter of a postage stamp sized front lawn.

When we got out, the cruiser's doors thumping shut got the dogs' attention. They ran to the edge of the yard, barking manically. Johnson didn't move a muscle, and didn't seem to have any intention of intervening. Ford made kissy noises and held his hand out to the dogs. They calmed and sniffed his hand. Before I knew what was happening, Ford had the dogs eating out of his hand, literally. He had had a couple dog treats concealed in his fist. He proceeded up the driveway with his two new best friends trotting at his side. I followed.

"Very good, Officer," Johnson said. He was barefoot in shorts and a T-shirt that said Up North across the chest. He had a white beard that was just a shade too long to be called groomed, and white hair that was also just a shade too long.

Ford introduced us and asked for a couple minutes of Johnson's time. Johnson waved a hand to two other lawn chairs set up in the garage. We sat, and the dogs took up positions at Ford's knees.

"We'd like to talk to you about the suicide your father witnessed in 1971," Ford said.

"I don't know anything about that," Johnson said.

"Your father told the police at the time that Peter Wilson stepped in front of that dump truck on purpose."

"Okay," Johnson said as if he couldn't have cared less.

"He said," Ford continued, "that Wilson was not pushed, did not trip, and appeared to be watching the truck coming down the road, and timed it so that he would step out in front of the truck, without leaving the driver time to stop."

"Sounds like you already know what my father saw," Johnson said.

"Was it the truth?" Ford said.

"Why wouldn't it be?" Johnson said.

I wanted to reach over and smack him upside the head. I knew he knew more than he was saying. "Did you go to Vietnam, Mr. Johnson?" I said

"No."

"Were you in college?"

"No."

"National Guard?"

"No."

"So how did you not get drafted?"

"Just lucky I guess."

"I understand that Captain Hannigan was in the habit of exchanging deferments for things."

"I wouldn't know anything about that," Johnson said.

"So you don't know if your father made a deal with The Captain?"

"I have no knowledge of any dealings between my father and The Captain."

"Just to be clear," I said, "your father did not give Captain Hannigan anything in exchange for a deferment for you?"

"You'd have to ask him."

"Your father's dead," Ford said.

"Maybe you can ask The Captain," Johnson suggested.

"Maybe we will," I said.

CHAPTER EIGHTEEN

When we got back to the downtown area, guys in orange mesh don't-run-me-over safety vests were in the middle of Michigan Avenue, setting up orange cones. Another group of men dressed the same had set up roadblocks across South Ann Arbor Street.

"What's going on over there?" I said.

"DPW guys are closing off that block for the Summerfest," Ford said.

"What's the Summerfest?"

Ford maneuvered the cruiser around the orange cones, and the guys dressed like orange cones, and then we headed back down Michigan Avenue towards my car. "It's not much," he said, "we just block off an area for a few days and have a little party. There will be some street vendors, a beer tent, and some of those food trailers. I think there's even going to be a gambling tent, like a Vegas night kind of thing, for charity. They also have this portable stage that they set up for entertainment; everything from the little girls' dance classes, to the school choirs, to karate demonstrations, to some half decent semi-professional rock bands."

"A lot of people show up?" I asked.

Ford nodded. "Yeah, actually, it's usually a pretty good time. I'll have to pull an extra shift or two, but I'll probably go when I'm off duty as well." He braked to a stop behind my Charger and slammed the cruiser into park. "So what's next?"

"I don't know," I admitted, pressing my palms into my eyes and my head into the headrest. The headache was mounting a counter-assault against the aspirin. "We need to find Carol Stockton, and it might help if we could get some more information on The Captain's deferment scam."

"What do you want me to do?"

"Find Carol Stockton."

"What are you going to do?"

"Find someone who can confirm the deferment scam."

CHAPTER NINETEEN

Rick Leland drove a big ass John Deere lawnmower. I didn't see much grass coming out of the chute, and I couldn't tell what part of the lawn he had mowed and what part he hadn't mowed. He made a precise 45° turn and saw me. He waved and stopped the machine. He made a big production of pulling levers and pushing buttons and the roar of the mower stopped.

He threw one leg over the steering wheel and climbed off. He wore his cutoff shorts and a tank top with a pair of work boots, mirrored sunglasses, and a straw hat that was somewhere between John Wayne's Stetson and my grandma's big floppy gardening hat.

"You again," he said, walking towards me.

"Me again," I said.

Leland took off the hat and wiped his forehead with the back of the same hand. He shook his head. "I already told you I don't have anything to say."

"I didn't ask you anything. I just came to take you up on that beer you offered."

Leland smiled a knowing smile. "All right then," he said, "come on."

He led me to a barn that sat behind the pole barn that he lived in. I chuckled at the irony of it. I really liked this guy. Leland pulled open the door to a refrigerator that sat just inside the door. It was lined wall-to-wall with cans of Pabst Blue Ribbon. He pulled out two cans with one hand, and tossed one of the cans to me all in one practiced motion.

I popped the tab and sucked off the foam that bubbled up through the hole. Then I took a drink and finished it with an exaggerated "ahh." Leland did the same, minus the ahh, never taking his skeptical gaze off of me.

"What's under the tarp," I said, gesturing towards what was obviously a vehicle covered by a tarp.

"A truck."

"You don't say. Can I see it?"

Leland set his beer on the ground and pulled the tarp off the front of the truck as if he was turning back bed covers. He revealed the cab and left the tarp lying across the bed of the truck. For someone who comes from the motor city, I know nothing about cars or trucks. All I knew about this one was that it had a white hood and a red body, was old, and said Ford across the front of it.

I took a guess. "Wow, a '64 Ford."

"'65," Leyland said.

Just missed. "Oh yeah, '65," I said.

Leland smiled that big droopy mustache smile of his. "Good guess," he said, picking up his beer.

I laughed. "I worked my way through college as the weight guessing guy at Cedar Point. I gave away a lot of key chains."

"My dad bought it when I was in high school," Leyland said gesturing to the truck. "It's about the only thing he owned that was worth any value, and he damn sure wasn't giving it to The Captain to keep my ass out of Vietnam. I hated this damn truck for a long time. It wasn't until after the old man died that I realized it wasn't about the truck. He lived his whole life in this town and didn't owe The Captain a damn thing, and neither do I."

"What did Randy Adams's family have?"

Leland shook his head slowly. "That's just the thing, his family had less than mine. They didn't even have a damn pickup truck to give to The Captain."

"So you really don't know," I said.

Leland finished off his beer and shook his head. "I really don't know."

CHAPTER TWENTY

Jerry Douglas sat behind a big chunky desk. He had small round brown frame glasses perched on a nose that sloped up at the end like a ski jump. He was clean shaven and his hair was more gray than brown, but the brown was fighting the good fight. His suit coat hung on a hanger on a peg mounted on the back of the closed door. The top button of his shirt was still done up and his tie was still high and tight. He had sent his secretary for coffee and was apparently waiting for her to return before speaking.

We were in an old two-story house on Michigan Avenue, a few blocks east of the downtown area. The old house, like several other houses along the main drag, had been converted into an office building. The former living room was the reception/waiting area. Douglas's office was in what I guessed was a dining room at one time. I assumed the kitchen was still the kitchen and that was where the secretary had gone to get the coffee.

I watched cars pass soundlessly by through the big windows that faced Michigan Avenue for a couple of minutes and then said, "Been here long?"

Rick Leland had pointed me towards Douglas and had called ahead to tell Douglas I was okay. He was deep in thought and my question startled him.

Yes," he said. "We've been in this building since the mid-80s. Before that we were downtown and one of the storefronts."

The office door opened and the secretary came through with a silver coffee pot and two china cups on a silver serving tray. She placed the tray on Douglas's desk and picked up the pot. Douglas stopped her. "That's okay, Tracy," he said. "I'll pour."

Tracy set the pot down and left the office. Douglas picked up the pot and poured coffee into the cups. "Do you take anything in it?"

"Black is fine," I said. "Thank you."

Douglas handed me the cup and said, "My father started this agency in the 40s."

"Is that right?"

"Saline was mostly a farming community back then, but he did well. He was honest and valued his clients. They in turn were loyal to the agency."

"And now?"

"We still have a pretty good customer base. You'd think that the Internet would drive our business down, but it really hasn't. We're a pretty tight knit community and the people are still loyal."

"Do you have much competition in town?"

"None."

I raise my eyebrows. "You're the only insurance agent in town?"

"Yes."

"Wow," I said.

"A few outside guys moved into town over the years, and set up shop, but they were unable to take our client base away. They all moved on to other towns and eventually competition stopped trying."

"You must be good."

Douglas shrugged. "I guess."

"Could there be another reason why people in this town are so loyal?"

"Such as?"

"I don't know. You tell me."

"I wouldn't know," Douglas said.

"Are you the sole owner of this business?" I asked.

Douglas didn't answer right away.

"The business records are public knowledge, Mr. Douglas. I can find out."

"I'm the agent," Douglas said, sounding defeated.

"But not the owner?"

Douglas shook his head. His eyes were cast on the desktop.

"The Captain?"

He nodded.

"How did he get his hooks in?"

"My father had fought in World War II. He never talked to me about it, until the war in Vietnam escalated, which happened to be right around the time I was graduating from high school. He did not want me to go to war."

"You went to college?" I said, pointing at the diploma from Michigan State University that hung on the wall behind his head. "You would have received a student deferment."

Douglas smiled dryly. "Maybe in other towns, but not here. Here you had to have something The Captain wanted, or you went to war. Your status didn't matter."

"Your father gave him the agency?"

"Only half at first. Then The Captain squeezed him out. I had no idea that my father had given him anything. Officially, I was on a student deferment. I didn't know that my father had bought the deferment until he died, and I found out that I was not inheriting the agency."

"He never told you?"

Douglas shook his head. "I guess he was too proud to admit that he gave away the thing he had spent his life building."

I let it hang for a moment. We both watched the traffic out the front window. I finally turned to Douglas. "I'm not a father," I said, "but I have no doubt that your father had no problem trading his business for your safety."

Douglas stared out the window for another full minute. He finally took a deep breath, let it out and turned back to me. "Thank you," he said.

I nodded. "What's your status here?"

"As I said, I'm the agent, officially licensed and legal, but The Captain owns the agency. I work on salary, same as Tracy, and the same as my father had. The Captain takes all the profits."

"How many other people did he do this to?"

"I don't know," Douglas said, shaking his head. "It's the town's dirty little secret. Nobody talks openly about it, but everybody knows."

"Did you know Randy Adams?"

Douglas nodded. "We went to school together. He was a year or two younger than me."

"You heard about the accident that killed him?"

"Of course. Nobody dies in this town, without everybody knowing it."

"Did you know Peter Wilson?"

"Yes."

"I know that Randy didn't go to Vietnam. Did Peter?"

"No."

"Did his parents give The Captain a business?"

"No."

"How did he buy his deferment?"

Douglas swiveled his chair and looked out the window. He tented his fingers and rested his chin on them. "I don't know for sure," he said.

"But you know something."

"Not everybody in this town bought deferments. Some people actually went to Vietnam."

"Like Rick Leland," I said.

Douglas smiled. "Rick's a good man. He's loving life these days, makes me wish I had gone to Vietnam and hadn't had this secret hanging over me my whole life, and my father's."

"Leland is not who you're referring to though, is he?"

"No. Another classmate of ours, Terry Graham, went off to war and was killed. A bunch of us went to his funeral. Afterwards we were hanging out and drinking beer and whatnot. We were all feeling pretty lousy for having stayed home while Terry went and died. Peter was really drunk, and really upset. I asked him what was making him so upset, other than the obvious. He told me that he had done something really horrible to get his deferment. Unforgivable, he said."

"This was after Peter had run down Randy?"

Douglas nodded.

"You think it wasn't an accident?"

Douglas swiveled his chair back to face me. "The Captain took out a life insurance policy on Randy Adams a week before the accident. $100,000, with a clause that paid double in the event that Randy died in an accident."

I stepped out into the heat of the parking lot to find what I was beginning to think of as my stalker, leaning his ass against the front fender of his police cruiser in his customary pose.

"Officer Ford," I said. "What a pleasant surprise."

"Mr. Chase," Ford said, very business-like, and then a smile spread out across his face.

"So what have you got?" I said.

"Jennifer London," he said, grinning like a lunatic.

"Okay, I'll bite. Who's Jennifer London?"

"She was Peter Wilson's girlfriend back in the day."

"Good job, Ford," I said, really meaning it. "Where do I find her?"

"We."

"We?"

"Where do we find her."

"Okay," I said. "Let's do it."

CHAPTER TWENTY-ONE

Jennifer London lived on a dairy farm west of town. The smell of a hundred or so cows hit me as soon as I got out of the car. A dog ran full tilt around the corner of the house, headed right at us. It pulled up when it got to me and stuck its nose in my crotch.

A woman's voice yelled, "Carl!" A whistle followed and the dog extracted its snout from my business and ran off.

I looked after the dog and saw the woman who had called it off. She was wearing the kind of short shorts that we called Daisy Dukes back in the eighties, a tank top that barely contained her above average breasts and a pair of rubber boots covered in cow shit. She glistened from sweat that collected on her chest and ran down her cleavage.

"Sorry about Carl," she said, walking toward us. "He's just saying hi."

"No problem," I said, managing to tear my eyes away from her cleavage. "I wish more people greeted me that way."

"Carl's not a people," the woman said laughing, "but I get your point."

"You wouldn't happen to be Jennifer London, would you?"

Another laugh. "Jennifer is my aunt. I'm—"

"Cissy," Ford said.

Cissy turned her attention to Ford. "That's right. Do I know you?"

"I'm Jim Ford," he said. "We went to high school together."

Cissy looked Ford up and down quizzically.

"I grew six inches after high school," Ford said.

"I see," Cissy said.

Ford dropped his eyes to the ground shyly and shrugged his shoulders. I hadn't seen this side of him before. It was interesting.

"Is your aunt here?" I said. "She's expecting us."

Cissy peeled her eyes off of Ford. "I think she's on the back porch."

The back porch spanned the width of the house, protruded ten or twelve feet and was covered by a roof. A lady with a helmet of gray hair and skin that looked like the leather bomber jacket I wore back in the eighties sat at a table beneath a slowly turning ceiling fan. She wore blue jeans, a sleeveless yellow shirt, and cow shit covered rubber boots, just like Cissy's.

"Aunt Jenny," Cissy said, "these are the men you were expecting."

"Ma'am," Ford said, bowing his head.

I introduced the two of us and thanked Aunt Jenny for agreeing to talk to us.

"Nonsense," she said. "I'm glad to do it."

Ford and I sat at the table and accepted the offer of lemonade. I let Ford take the lead as we had agreed while driving out to the farm.

"I understand you knew Peter Wilson," he said.

Aunt Jenny's face lit up. "Oh my, yes," she said. "I was just a dumb kid, but did I ever love him."

"Can you tell us about him?"

"Well, what do you want to know?"

"Obviously we want to know about the accidents; the one when he was driving and the other one when he was not."

"There's not much to tell about the first one. We were supposed to go to the movies that night. Peter was on his way to pick me up when that man darted out in front of him. Peter didn't have a chance to avoid him."

"Is that what Peter told you?" I asked. "That he didn't have a chance to avoid him?"

She scowled at me. "What are you implying?"

"I'm not implying anything," I said. "I'm just trying to make sure I have the facts straight. Did Peter tell you he didn't have a chance, or did you infer it?"

"He told me," she said.

"How did he react to the accident?" Ford asked calmly.

Aunt Jenny held her glare on me for another few seconds and then slowly turned her attention back to Ford. "He took it hard. He was a really sweet young man. He wouldn't hurt anyone intentionally. As a matter of fact, he was struggling to decide what to do if he got drafted. He wanted to run to Canada, but his dad was really pressuring him to go to Vietnam."

"Couldn't he have gone to college and gotten a deferment?" I asked.

I knew she heard me but she didn't look at me. To Ford she said, "He wouldn't have been able to go to college because his family couldn't afford it."

"How did he get a deferment?" I asked.

"I don't like you," she said to me.

I raised my eyebrows and leaned toward her. "Would it surprise you if I told you that he told somebody else that he had done something horrible to get his deferment?"

"What would that be?"

"I don't know. I was hoping that you might?"

"Well I don't."

"Do you think he killed himself?" Ford asked, again breaking the tension between Aunt Jenny and me.

"No way," she said.

"He wasn't distraught about having run down Randy?"

"He was for a long time, but he was doing much better. He was at peace with what had happened. If he had died a few months earlier I might have believed it, but not then. He was doing much better. We were talking about the future for the first time in a long time. Then one day he was dead. The police said he stepped in front of a dump truck and died the same way he had killed Randy Adams."

CHAPTER TWENTY-TWO

Ford pulled the car to the side of the road and slammed it into park. Corn stalks filled the fields on both sides of us. It felt like we were in the middle of a Children of the Corn movie. I expected Malachi to jump out with a butcher's knife.

The big man turned in his seat, as much as the seat would allow, and looked at me. "You want to tell me what's going on here?"

I hesitated and looked out the windshield. "I don't know if I'm ready," I said.

"Bullshit," Ford said. "I'm putting my job on the line having anything to do with you. The least you can do is to tell me what it is we're doing?"

I took a breath and then spilled it. "I think The Captain used deferments to build his little empire here. I also think that his daughter Meredith is not really his daughter. I think his real daughter died and he replaced her with a baby that he traded a deferment to Randy Adams for. I think Randy was a drug addict that The Captain didn't think he could trust, so he traded a deferment to Peter Wilson to kill Randy Adams, so that Randy couldn't talk. I'm not sure at this point if Peter really committed suicide over it, or if The Captain had him killed as well."

Ford sat quietly while I spilled my guts. He took a moment to take it all in and then said, "So how do we prove all this?"

I was surprised. "You're in?"

"Yeah," Ford said. "I know you think everybody in this town is bent, or beholden to the Hannigans, but we're not. As a matter of fact, most of us are tired of dealing with them. If we can prove what you just said, I think we can finally take our town back."

He drove me back to my car. Along the way I told Ford about the beating I had taken and told him to watch his ass.

"Where are you going?" he said as I climbed out of the car.

"To talk to the nurse."

CHAPTER TWENTY-THREE

The giant sorority house was empty, and hotter than hell. Since there were no residents during the summer the sorority didn't feel the added expense of air conditioning was necessary, or at least that was how Carol Stockton explained it to me.

She invited me into her house director apartment. A small window air conditioner worked overtime to take of the edge off the heat. It wasn't a lot, but it was enough to make the space bearable. The glass full of iced tea that sat before me on the coffee table sweated profusely.

"Been here long?" I asked.

"Just a few years," Mrs. Stockton answered, "since I retired from the hospital. It gives me a place to live and a small income to supplement my social security."

"How is it living with a house full of college girls?"

"They're a pain in the ass," she said conspiratorially. I laughed. "But it's better than living in a house full of people waiting to die."

"Anyway," I said, "I need to ask you about Meredith Hannigan."

"I don't really know anything about Meredith Hannigan."

"I was told that you were working at the hospital when she was born."

Mrs. Stockton said, "Okay. When was that?"

"1969."

"1969?" she said. "How am I supposed to remember –"

"Come on Mrs. Stockton," I said, cutting off her feigned ignorance. "Everybody in Saline remembers everything there is to do with the Hannigans; especially Meredith, the miracle baby."

"I just—"

"Please. You can help me save a young woman's life."

"I'm sure you're just being dramatic."

"No, I'm not," I said. Then I told Mrs. Stockton the whole story. I told her of Caroline Wolf and the baby she had at Woodstock. I told her about Randy Adams and his telling Caroline Wolf that the baby died and he buried it and then about his statement to Rick Leland about having something The Captain wanted. "Could Meredith Hannigan be Caroline Wolf's baby?"

Mrs. Stockton listened to every word I said without interrupting. When I finished she was looking out the window. In a quiet voice she said, "Meredith was born premature. She weighed barely two pounds, and had a number of other complications. The doctors wanted to transfer her to St. Joes in Ann Arbor, but The Captain wouldn't hear of it. He insisted they keep her in Saline."

"Why?"

"I don't know. All I know is we kept her. She stayed in an incubator for several weeks. I didn't think she was going to make it. A priest was even called in and administered Last Rites."

"But she made it."

Mrs. Stockton nodded her head. "I went into work one day and she was fine. She was fattened up, and she had good color. All her complications had been overcome."

"Just like that," I said.

"The Captain and Mrs. Hannigan took her home the next day."

CHAPTER TWENTY-FOUR

I called an old acquaintance that I had met at a few Police Officers Association of Michigan events. When we had met years before he had been a detective with the Ann Arbor Police. He was the chief of police in Ann Arbor now.

"Warner," he said rather gruffly when he answered.

"Lou?" I said. "It's Tyson Chase."

"Chase?" he said, only slightly softer. "What the hell do you want?"

I laughed. "I want to buy you a drink."

"You can do that at the next POAM dinner."

"No, I can't," I said. "I'm no longer a member."

"Did you finally get fired?"

"Not fired, exactly. I was encouraged to retire."

It was Warner's turn to laugh. "Finally went too far, huh?'

"It was politics."

"That's what they all say."

"Yeah, maybe," I said. "So how about that drink?"

I heard pages turning while I waited for Warner to respond. He obviously was looking through an appointment book. By the number of pages I heard turn I didn't think it was going to happen.

"Ah screw it," he finally said. "I have a dinner I have to be at tonight, but I can give you ten minutes in the bar before I make my appearance. Will that work?"

"That should be fine," I said. "Thanks Lou."

"Yeah. See you later," he said, and then the line went dead.

CHAPTER TWENTY-FIVE

The Catholic Church in town was named for St. Andrew. There happened to be confession that evening. Since I had some time before my meeting with Warner, I hoped to get a word in with the priest while I waited.

I grew up Catholic, was even an altar boy, but hadn't stepped foot in a church since I was sixteen years old. I hoped I didn't burn up on re-entry. I automatically dipped my fingers in the holy water font and made the sign of the cross. The sanctuary was beautiful, dominated with wood and brick and a tiled floor. The pews wrapped around in a semi-circle. I looked around for the telltale red light that would signify that the priest was sitting in the confessional. I found it in the back corner of the sanctuary. I sat in a nearby pew waiting for him to come out.

The confessional door opened and Michael Hannigan, the police chief, exited. I hit my knees and bowed my head, hoping he hadn't seen my face. He looked too self-absorbed to have noticed me if I had been naked and on fire. I waited for what seemed an eternity while he knelt and prayed his penance. I wondered if my being in town had stirred up old sins from which he now sought absolution, or if he was working on a new batch of sins. He finally crossed himself, stood and left the sanctuary. Again he didn't look around him. Most cops know what is going on around them at all times. For Hannigan to not see me must have meant that he was totally into his own world.

Nobody else entered the church and eventually the priest came out of the confessional. He saw me immediately and said, "Are you here for confession, Son?"

He was rather tall with a shock of thick white hair and bushy white eyebrows. He wore black pants, a black short sleeve shirt and his clerical collar. Priest casual, I had called the look in my youth. He carried a purple stole and a small bible in his hands.

"No Father," I said. "But I would like to talk to you, if you have a couple minutes."

"Of course," he said in a soft but commanding voice. He walked to the pew where I sat and extended his hand. "I'm Father Steven Williams."

I shook his hand and introduced myself. He sat in the pew, turned toward me with his right leg crossed over his left knee.

He smiled and said, "So what do you need to talk about?"

"The Hannigans." The smile slowly melted from his face. "You've been here a long time?" I said before he could say anything.

"A few years," he said. "The Bishop moves us around from time to time."

"So you weren't here when Meredith Hannigan was born?" I said.

The smile returned and a wave of relief crossed his face. "No."

"But you know her story."

"Yes, of course."

"She was given Last Rites in the hospital?"

"That's my understanding."

"Do you know who gave her the last rites?"

"That would have been Father Jefferies. He was the parish priest back then."

"Is Father Jefferies still around?"

The priest hesitated. "He's retired."

"Do they have an old retired priest's home they send them to, or something like that?"

"I'm sorry, but I can't tell you."

"Can't, or won't?"

"Can't. It is against the rules."

I laughed. "Okay, Father," I said. "When I find him I won't tell him you ratted him out."

I walked to my car and pulled my cell phone out. Sarge answered on the first ring. "Were you sitting on the phone or something?" I asked. It was a cordless phone and most of the time we couldn't find it to answer it.

"Nope," Sarge said with a hint of pride in his voice, "it was right where it was supposed to be."

"How'd that happen?"

"Sally."

"Sally?"

"Yep," Sarge said. "She's got this place organized like you wouldn't believe. Did you know we had a blender?"

"No way," I said.

"Way," Sarge said. "Sally found it."

"Well I'll be damned," I said. "Speaking of Sally, is she there? Can I talk to her for a minute?"

"Why?" Sarge said, playing the over-protective uncle.

"Just put her on the phone, Sarge."

The line went quiet for a minute and then Sally said, "Hey, Chase. What's up?"

"Hey, Sally," I said, "good work on the blender."

"Really?" Sally said. "You're telling me you didn't know you had a blender?"

"Look around. It's not like we're catering to the pina colada crowd."

She chuckled. "You two run this place like…"

"Like a couple cops who have no business running a bar?"

"Yeah, that."

It was my turn to chuckle. "The reason I called," I said, "is I need a favor. Remember when you tracked down Steve Belloti for me? You think you could do that with a retired priest?"

"Sure," Sally said. "What's his name?"

"I don't want to put you out or anything. I think these guys go into like the witness protection program or something when they retire."

"If he's still using his name, I'll find him."

So I told Sally everything I knew about Father Jefferies, which wasn't much. She promised to have the info for me ASAP. I disconnected the call and laughed. A blender, who knew?

CHAPTER TWENTY-SIX

The bar at Weber's Inn was dark and crowded. I sat at the bar, drinking a beer and watching the Tigers game play silently on the widescreen TV mounted on the wall behind the bar. I was very much underdressed in my tee shirt and jeans. The rest of the patrons wore tuxedos and evening gowns. Warner came in wearing his dress blue uniform. He had braids on the shoulders and shiny gold medals that matched his shiny gold badge. I stood up and saluted.

He didn't return the salute. "Don't be a jackass," he said. He got the bartender's attention and ordered Wild Turkey on the rocks. He waited for the drink. When it came he took about half of it in a single pull and then set the glass on the bar. Then he looked at me. "What do you want?"

"What can you tell me about Captain Hannigan?" I said.

"Captain," Warner snorted. "Fuck him. Slimy little fuck."

"Don't hold back," I said, "tell me what you really think."

Warner finished the Wild Turkey and rapped the glass on the bar to get the bartender's attention. "What do you want me to say?" he said after the bartender had refilled the glass.

I told Warner that I thought Hannigan had replaced his dying child with The Woodstock Baby and had killed two people to cover it up. "Do you think he's capable of something like that?"

"Hell yes, he's capable of something like that," Warner said.

"Will you help me nail him?"

"Nope."

"Why   not?"

Warner drained half the new glass of Wild Turkey. "Were you absent the day they taught jurisdiction at the academy?" he said. "I'd love to nail him, but I can't touch him."

"What do you suggest I do?"

"I'd tell you to go to the sheriff, but I think he's in bed with Hannigan. The state police won't do dick, they'll tell you to go to the sheriff. So what I'd do is go straight to the prosecutor. If you can convince him of your story, which by the way is just this side of Bigfoot, he'll help you. He's been dying for a chance to hang Hannigan's head on his wall."

"Can you give me an introduction?" I said.

"Call his office tomorrow. He'll be expecting you."

"Thanks, Lou."

Warner slammed down the rest of his drink and thumped the glass on the bar. "Yeah," he said. "I gotta get in there."

"Have fun," I said.

"I hate these fucking things," he said and trudged out of the bar.

I left the bar and headed back to Detroit. I got out of the Charger and heard a roar erupt from Comerica Park. I hustled into O'Ryan's amid a chorus of amazed "Holy Shit"s and "Did you see that?"s coming from our patrons.

"What happened?" I asked Sarge.

"Miggy just hit one to Timbuktu," Sarge said without taking his eyes off the TV.

"I missed it?" I said.

"Missed what?" Sally said, setting a beer and a manila folder in front of me.

"Miggy's homerun."

"Who's Miggy?"

Sarge finally peeled his eyes from the TV and fixed them on his niece. "Who's Miggy?"

Sally laughed. "Miguel Cabrera. Detroit Tigers third baseman. Hit .330 with 44 home runs and 139 runs batted in 2012 to win the first triple crown since Yaz in 67. That Miggy?"

"Yeah," Sarge said. "That Miggy."

If Sally's baseball knowledge didn't make me fall in love with her, what I found in the folder did. "This is great," I said. "Where'd you get this?"

Sally beamed with pride. "I can't tell you my secrets. A girl has to have some mystery."

"Sally used to work as a paralegal in a law firm," Sarge said. "Research was her specialty. What'd she get ya?"

"Well, not only did she find the priest, but according to this, he paid cash for a lake house valued at a quarter million."

"Where's a priest get a quarter mil to buy a house?" Sarge said.

"Would you like to tell him, Sally?" I said.

Sally grinned. Her white teeth sparkled. "Well," she said, "I wondered the same thing, so I called a guy I dated in college who happens to work for the IRS. I asked him to do some research for me and he discovered that Chase's Captain Hannigan wrote off the exact same amount as a charitable contribution on his taxes that same year."

"No way," Sarge said.

"Way," I said and high-fived Sally.

CHAPTER TWENTY-SEVEN

Warner was true to his word. I called the Washtenaw County Prosecutor's office the next morning. The lady who answered the phone said, "Yes, Mr. Chase, Mr. Preston just got off the phone with Chief Warner. He can see you right after lunch."

Since I had the morning free I decided to have a talk with Caroline Wolf. I hoped it wouldn't be horrible. I hoped she'd go along with my plan.

Her daughter was at the U of M Cancer Center, which happened to be in Ann Arbor, the same as the Washtenaw County Prosecutor. I found her sitting in a chair in the corner of the hospital room. She was reading while her daughter slept restlessly in the bed. I tapped softly on the door jamb. Caroline Wolf looked up from her reading and smiled. She put a finger to her lips to shush me and pointed out the door. I stepped back into the hall and she followed, pulling the door shut behind her.

"Hello, Mr. Chase," she said pleasantly.

"Mrs. Wolf," I said. "Can we get a cup of coffee or something?"

"Sure," she said. She led me down the hall.

"How's your daughter doing?"

"She's holding her own. But the longer it takes to find a donor the worse her chances are. Every day that she waits, her chance of survival drops."

I nodded, feeling like a shit. We walked in silence to the cafeteria. I bought two coffees and we sat at a table by the window.

"Are you making progress?" Caroline Wolf asked.

I sipped my coffee and nodded my head. "I think so. I've spent the past few days in Randy Adams's hometown. There was some pretty hinky stuff going on back in the sixties and seventies."

"Such as?"

"I think I told you that the guy who ran the local draft board is rumored to have traded deferments for cash, pieces of businesses, pretty much anything that caught his eye."

"Right, you mentioned that. I think you called him The Captain."

"Right, The Captain."

"Does he have my child?" Caroline Wolf asked. She had scooted to the front edge of her chair. He eyes were expectant.

"I don't know," I said. "He does have a daughter that is about the same age. She was very sick when she was born, and then one day she was well."

"Can we talk to her? What's her name?" Her voice was bubbling.

"Her name is Meredith. I have no idea if she knows anything about any of this. I would be very surprised if she has ever once thought about the possibility of being The Woodstock Baby."

"So you think she is?"

I took a breath and let it out slowly. "I think there is a possibility." Caroline Wolf started to speak and I cut her off. "Wait," I said. "I think there is more going on here than just Randy Adam s trading your baby for a deferment. I think, if he did it, he was murdered to cover it up. And, the person who killed him was killed as well."

Caroline Wolf sat back in her chair. Her expectant eyes turned solemn. "And?" she said.

"I have a meeting this afternoon with the Washtenaw County Prosecutor. I want to see if he will pursue it. If Sara needs the transplant today I will try to talk to Meredith Hannigan, but if you think she can hang on for a little bit, I'd really like to pursue the murder angle. It's your call."

She looked at me. I could tell she wanted me to go straight to Meredith Hannigan and ask her to donate bone marrow to her long lost sister, but she sighed and said, "I think Sara is okay for a little bit."

It was the answer I had hoped for.

"A very little bit, Mr. Chase," she said.

CHAPTER TWENTY-EIGHT

I had never met Gerald Preston and knew nothing about him except that he wasn't a fan of The Captain. I wasn't a fan of The Captain either, so we went into the meeting with at least one thing in common.

He was a bear of a man. He towered over me and his hand, when we shook, was like sticking my hand into a black hole. He wasn't fat, in the sense that he didn't have a belly hanging over his belt, but he was thick and well filled out. He wore a beard that needed a trim and his hair was cut in a don't-give-a-shit way. My first impression was that of a man who should have been wearing blue jeans and a flannel shirt with the sleeves cut off, not a suit and tie.

"Mr. Chase," he said when he shook my hand. His voice sounded like James Earl Jones, only deeper.

I thanked him for agreeing to see me and sat in the chair he indicated.

"Chief Warner suggested I meet with you," he said, sitting in a throne sized chair behind his desk. "He said you might be of some help in dealing with Captain Hannigan."

"I do have an interest in The Captain," I said.

"Are you a police officer?"

"Retired from the Detroit Police."

"Private eye then?"

"No sir, I own a bar."

"So you have no legal standing to be investigating anyone," Preston said, eyeing me skeptically.

"I guess not," I admitted.

"What's your interest in Hannigan?"

"I'm doing a favor for a nice lady who used to teach third grade. Hanningan's shenanigans came to my attention in the course of doing this favor."

"And what's the favor?"

"I'm trying to find her long lost child, the one she gave birth to at Woodstock."

"Woodstock?"

"Yes sir."

"The Woodstock?"

"Yes sir."

"Three days of peace and love and all that shit?"

I chuckled. "I felt the exact same way when she told me," I said. "I think I said almost the exact same words."

"You believe her?"

"I do," I said, nodding. "I was skeptical at first, but her story checks out, and I believe I have found the child. I also ran across information that leads me to believe that Captain Hannigan illegally gained custody of the child and has killed, or had killed, at least two people to cover it up."

Preston rocked back in his giant chair and scratched at his beard while he thought. "Who do you think it is?"

"Meredith Hannigan."

"The mayor?"

"Yes," I said.

Preston nodded. "She'd be about the right age, wouldn't she?"

"Exactly the right age."

"And it might explain the whole 'miracle baby' bullshit," Preston said. Apparently he wasn't a fan of the mayor either, or her story. "You think she knows?"

"I doubt it," I said. "It's not the sort of thing you tell your kid. I don't think her mother even knew. From what I understand, she was a big believer in the 'miracle baby' story."

"So what do you want from me?"

"Help."

CHAPTER TWENTY-NINE

Help came about an hour later. I was sitting in the coffee shop on the first floor of the Washtenaw County Courthouse. Somehow, the coffee shop was old and dingy in a building that was pretty clean and modern. I was trying to figure out how it could have happened – did they build the building around the coffee shop? – when a gorgeous woman in a form fitting black dress that stopped mid-thigh entered. She wore a blazer over the dress, but it did nothing to hide an incredible body. She looked around briefly, spotted me and walked over.

"Chase?" she said.

I nodded, trying not to stare at the cleavage that bubbled out of the dress.

"Julie Runyan," she said, sliding into the booth across from me. She placed a manila file folder on the table between us.

"Pleased to meet you," I said and smiled.

"Gerald assigned me to you."

"Gerald?"

"Gerald Preston? The County Prosecutor?"

"Oh, that Gerald," I said.

"Everybody in the office calls him Gerald," Julie said, reading my mind. "He insists on it. Anyway, he told me to give you whatever you want."

I raised my eyebrows.

She gave me a look that I've seen far too many times and said, "Don't even think about it."

I laughed and the awkwardness left. Julie pushed the manila folder towards me with her finger.

"The birth certificate is legit," she said.

I flipped open the folder and pulled the certificate toward me. Meredith Leigh Hannigan was born July 2, 1969 to Ruth and Leslie Hannigan.

"Leslie?" I said. "No wonder he wants everyone to call him The Captain."

Julie rolled her eyes at me. "Anyway," she said in an exaggerated way. "I have to get back to the office. If you need anything else call me."

"Wait," I said. She stopped half way out of the booth. "I assumed the birth certificate would be legit. My contention is that they switched the baby out."

"And did what with the real Meredith Hannigan?"

"I don't know. Threw it in the trash for all I know. "

"So what do you want?"

I was almost positive that Meredith Hannigan was the Woodstock Baby, but I had no proof. The logical way to prove it would be a DNA sample. The only hang-up to that plan was getting the DNA from Meredith. "I want to get a DNA sample."

"So ask her for one."

"Really? What would you say if some stranger walked into your office and asked you for a DNA sample?"

"I'd tell him to get lost," Julie said.

I threw both of my hands at her, palms up, in a there-you-go gesture.

"Okay," Julie said, "but we need probable cause to get a warrant. You have heard of probable cause, right? Or don't they use that in Detroit?"

CHAPTER THIRTY

I sat in my car on the side of Harris St, about 100 yards down from the City Hall/Police Department. I was watching the BMW SUV that was parked in the spot reserved for the mayor. It was after five and I hoped that she wouldn't be much longer. I didn't enjoy stakeouts, and it was still very hot and humid.

A tall woman with impossibly long legs sprouting from under a dark blue skirt exited the building. She carried a purse and a large bag over her right shoulder. She pointed what must have been her key fob at the SUV with her left hand because the lights flashed once; a sure sign of any car being locked or unlocked. She opened the back door first and dumped her carry-ons on the back seat, and then climbed into the driver's seat and started the car.

I backed my car into a side street, ready to pull out and head in whichever direction the mayor went. She turned right out of the parking lot and drove past me. I gave her a head start and then followed. There was enough traffic for me to keep two or three cars between us, but not enough for me to lose her. She led me past the public library and the middle school to a subdivision of impressive houses.

She turned into a driveway of a two-story modern brick home with more roof angles than I could count on first sight. The yard was huge and the perfectly manicured grass was so green, given the heat wave, I thought it might have been fake. I cruised slowly past the house and watched as the garage door on the two car section of the three car garage went up and the mayor drove the Beemer in. I didn't want to take anything for granted, but I figured if she was parking in the garage, it must be her house.

I drove past the house and did a turn-around in the driveway of a house around the bend where the mayor wouldn't be able to see me. I then cruised slowly back the way I had come, and stopped where I could watch the house, without being obvious that I was doing so. I didn't think it was the sort of neighborhood where one could sit undisturbed on the side of the road for long. My hypothesis was confirmed when a police car pulled into the subdivision and rolled to a stop window to window with my car. I put my window down as the cop car did the same.

"I should have known it was you," Chief Hannigan said, shaking his head.

"How'd you get onto me so fast?"

"Meredith called and said she had someone following her."

"She did?" I said. "It was a five minute ride."

"She had a stalker a couple years back so she is very aware of her surroundings. Being the mayor gets her pretty fast service."

"From the chief no less," I said.

"What are you doing here?" Hannigan said, ignoring my comment.

"House hunting," I said. "This seems to be a nice community. I'm thinking about moving here."

"You're harassing my family," the chief said.

"The only person in your family that I've talked to, is you."

"You've been asking questions about my father. Why?"

"I'm curious," I said. "The more I hear about the infamous Captain, the curiouser I get."

"My father doesn't like people asking questions about him."

I rubbed the back of my head. It was still sore. "I'm aware of that."

"You need to go back to Detroit, and leave this alone," Hannigan said, "before somebody gets hurt."

He wore sunglasses, and I couldn't see his eyes to get a read on him. Was he threatening me? Or was he trying to warn me? Either way, I had never been one to be scared off. It was why Caroline Wolf had asked me to look into this.

"When did you become chief of police?" I asked.

"Long time ago," the chief said with a sigh.

"What are you, 62, 63? Planning to retire soon?"

"Someday."

"You go college?"

"U of M."

"Go blue," I said. "Is that how you stayed out of Vietnam? Student deferment?"

"Yes."

"What did you buy the deferment with?"

Hannigan's eyebrows rose behind the dark lenses. "Excuse me?"

"I asked you what you used to buy your deferment," I said, staring into the dark lenses. "From what I hear, your father wouldn't just give a deferment. You had to buy it."

"Whoever told you that was lying," Hannigan said, sounding like a little kid on the playground. "My dad never took bribes."

I smirked. "Maybe you didn't know about them, but I'm sure it happened."

Hannigan shook his head. "Just leave it alone."

"Tell me about your sister."

"What?"

I looked away from the chief and at his sister's house. "Your sister, Meredith."

"Go home, Mr. Chase," the police chief said. "Whatever did or didn't happen a long time ago is none of your business. I know you think you're doing a good thing, but believe me, no good will come from this. Just go home and leave it alone."

I dropped the Charger into drive and said, "I can't do that, Chief," and drove away.

If I was right about Meredith, then I had just blown my cover. Getting DNA from her now was going to be just about impossible. "Good going, Chase," I said.

CHAPTER THIRTY-ONE

I sat in an Adirondack chair on the deck of Father Jefferies' lake house. The sun, a giant ball of flame, sent shafts of orange light bouncing across the lake as it slowly made its descent into the horizon. A breeze skipped across the swells of water and washed over us. It was the first hint of fresh air I had felt in weeks. It felt so good to sit there and feel the breeze and watch the sunset I almost forgot why I was there to begin with.

"This is amazing Father," I said.

The old priest sat in a matching chair, angled just right so that two people could converse, but still take in the view of the lake. He had about 13 gray hairs scattered about the top of his head with a horseshoe of matching hair ringing the back and sides. Smooth skin that looked as if it had never been shaved hung loose from his jaw, as if his face was sliding off his skull. He wore a red and white Hawaiian shirt, khaki pants, and brown sandals. I had noticed a tremor in his hand when he had handed me a glass of iced tea. I figured it was either Parkinson's, or just the fact that he was about 157 years old.

"Yes," he said with a smile, "I have truly been blessed."

"I wanted to talk to you about the Hannigan's," I said, and watched the smile fade.

"Oh, uh, sure. I don't know what I can tell you though. They were one of the families in my parish, but I didn't really know them very well."

"Come on Father. Everybody knows the Hannigan's."

"Well, sure."

"I'm especially interested in Meredith," I said. "I'd really like to hear your version of her birth, and her time in the hospital."

The tremor in the priest's hand increased. Ice rattled in his glass. He set it on the table between us. "Well--"

"From what I hear, you gave her the last rites, and then the next day she was healed."

The old man was visibly rattled. "Well, I wouldn't say--"

"You performed a miracle, Father. Isn't that the first step to sainthood? Performing a miracle?"

"Now wait a minute--"

"The Bishop knows about this, right? And the Cardinal?"

"The Bishop? What?"

"I don't know how it works though. Do we have to get the Pope involved? Is it the Pope that makes someone a saint?"

The poor old man shook uncontrollably. "Wh...what? Wait. Stop."

"Isn't that the way it happened?" I said, cocking my head to the side, quizzically.

Father Jeffries took a couple of ragged breaths and dropped his chin to his chest. "No," he said, shaking his head slowly. "No, that's not how it happened."

I looked away and watched the sun slip slowly into oblivion while the priest got himself together. I felt horrible about bullying the old man. "You want to tell me about it?"

I wasn't sure he had heard me. He stared at the lake, deep in thought.

"I haven't been to church in a while," I said, "but isn't there more than just going to confession and saying ten Hail Marys? Don't you have to make amends or something?"

Still nothing.

"This is your opportunity, Father. I'm trying to save a woman's life. I—"

"I did it for Ruth," he said, still not looking at me.

"Ruth?"

"Mrs. Hannigan. The Captain's wife. She was truly one of this world's kind souls. She had two sons that were in their teens when she got pregnant with Meredith. The doctors didn't think she was able to get pregnant. Meredith was a miracle long before she was born. Ruth was put on bed rest somewhere in her sixth month. She was very excited and desperately wanted a daughter.

"She was devastated when Meredith was born so sick. She thought it was her fault. The doctors didn't think Meredith was going to make it. She was in an incubator for a month. I administered the last rites three times. The third time was when we made the switch.

"I never would have done it if I had thought that Ruth would have been able to deal with losing her, but I didn't. I couldn't stand to see that wonderful woman in such pain."

"Where'd the baby come from?" I said.

"I don't know," the priest said, "I swear. The Captain approached me with the idea. He said he had a baby and wanted me to swap it out."

"And you just said yes?"

Father Jefferies shook his head. "No, I did not just say yes. I prayed about it and I sat with Ruth and we prayed together."

"Did she know about the switch?"

"No, absolutely not. She really thought Meredith had been touched by God."

"So God told you to make the switch?"

The old man finally looked at me. "No, Mr. Chase," he said with bite in his voice, "God did not tell me to make the switch, and I resent the sarcasm. I made the decision all on my own. As I said, I did it for Ruth, for her well-being. I guess I didn't think about how it would hurt other people."

"Well, Father," I said with a sigh, "it probably didn't hurt anybody, at least if the baby came from where I hope it came from."

CHAPTER THIRTY-TWO

It was late when I got back to the D. I was exhausted and still dealing with the effects of the hit on the head. I decided to skip O'Ryan's and go straight to bed. I parked at the curb in front of the bond office next door to O'Ryan's, and was just about to mount the outside stairs to my apartment when I was grabbed from behind and shoved face first against the wall of the bar. Hands reached around me from behind and groped at my crotch. I felt hot breath from ragged breathing in my ear.

"You owe me," a hoarse voice whispered in my ear.

A kiss was planted on my neck. The hands returned to my shoulders and spun me around. I caught a brief view of Trudy's face before she planted a kiss on my mouth. Suddenly, I didn't feel as tired.

CHAPTER THIRTY-THREE

I got a late start the next day. Trudy kept me up, literally and figuratively, most of the night. It was noon by the time I got started. I ventured into Ann Arbor to find Judy Wilde, the other lady in the VW on the trip to and from Woodstock. Sally had tracked her to an open-air vegetable stand in Ann Arbor. It was set up in the parking lot of a huge Salvation Army store on State Street, just south of the Michigan campus. I could see the enormous scoreboards that rose into the sky from the football stadium nicknamed The Big House, as I got out of the car.

I wandered toward the rows of fruits and vegetables, wondering how long they would stay good in the heat. I was approached by a young lady in a skin tight tank top and even tighter short shorts, which she pulled out of her crotch when she stopped walking.

"Anything I can help you find?" she asked.

I suppressed the urge to offer to take her into the Salvation Army and help her find some clothes that fit. Instead I asked for Judy Wilde.

The girl turned and scanned the area. She pointed to an older woman wearing a tie-dyed tee shirt, a long denim skirt and a pair of those rubber shoes they call crocs. She wore a floppy straw hat over gray hair that hung in a long single braid down her back.

"Finally," I murmured, "a hippie."

I thanked the young lady and headed toward Judy Wilde. She looked up as I approached and shielded her eyes from the sun as she looked up at me. I hadn't been able to tell from across the food co-op, but she wasn't even five feet tall.

"Ms. Wilde?" I said, offering my hand.

"That's right," she said, not taking my hand. "And who might you be?" I felt a bit of chill in the air, and not the good kind.

"My name is Chase," I said. "I'm—"

"A police officer," she said.

I chuckled. "Is it that obvious?"

"Right out of Central Casting, as they say."

I laughed at that. "Well, I'm not a police officer anymore. I own a bar in Detroit."

"Um hmm. And what are you doing this far from home."

"I'm actually doing a favor for a nice lady who used to be an acquaintance of yours. Caroline Wolf."

"I don't know a Caroline Wolf, Mr. Chase." She emphasized the mister as if she wanted to call me something else.

"She was the pregnant girl who rode to Woodstock with you and Steve Belloti."

"Steve Belloti," she said. "I haven't thought of him in a hundred years. I wonder what he's up to these days?"

"He's a lawyer in Southfield," I said. "I talked to him just the other day."

"A lawyer? So he sold out, huh?"

"Not necessarily. He represents union workers against the companies they work for."

That brought a knowing smile to Ms. Wilde's face. "As I recall, his parents were both union members. His hero was Walter Reuther."

It was my turn to smile. I had been right about Belloti.

"So what are you doing for Caroline?" Her tone seemed to warm a bit. Maybe the thought of Belloti fighting "the man" put her in a good mood.

"I'm trying to find her child. The one she had at Woodstock."

"Do you think I have it?"

"No, not at all," I said. "I'm just hoping you can help us fill in some blanks. Do you know anything about what happened to the baby?"

"Of course not. All I know is that she was pregnant on the way to the concert and not on the way back."

"You didn't ask her where the baby was?"

"Nope."

"Come on," I said. "Her not having the baby on the way home had to be the only thing that anybody in that van thought about all the way home."

Judy Wilde shook her head. "I'm telling you, we didn't talk about it. Caroline was a little quiet, but I thought she was just stoned."

"So you never saw the baby or heard anything about its disappearance?"

"No sir."

I was disappointed. I had really hoped she would know something. I thanked her and walked back to the car. I was just about to pull out of the lot when I saw Judy Wilde coming toward me, waving that big floppy hat. I stopped the car and rolled the window down.

"I haven't thought about this in 40 years," she said, "but I just remembered something."

"Anything you remember could help," I said.

She rested her hand on the window opening and leaned on it. "I did see a baby," she said.

"You did?"

She nodded her head vigorously. "The first day of the concert. I went back to the van to get something, I don't even remember what now, but as I walked back to the concert a young man was walking the other way, away from the concert, and he had a baby wrapped in a towel. I guess with all the hoopla of the next two days, what with the music and the rain and all the drugs, I forgot about it. But I remember thinking what's that boy doing walking down the side of the road with a baby wrapped in a towel?"

"Do you remember what he looked like?"

She squinted up her face. "Not really. I just remember that he didn't fit in at Woodstock. He was clean shaven and had his hair cut real short. And he was wearing chinos and like a sport shirt, short sleeved from what I could see under the towel."

"Would you recognize him if you saw him again?"

"I doubt it. It was forty years ago."

"Would you look at some pictures if I brought them back?"

She laughed. "Yep, you're a cop."

"Sorry," I said.

"I'm here every day," she said and turned and walked away.

CHAPTER THIRTY-FOUR

I sat in the Charger outside a bar called The Captain's Den, trying to decide if I was dumb enough to go in. It was obvious that this particular establishment was owned by The Captain, of course it would have been a good bet that he owned it anyway, even if it didn't have his name on it. What stopped me was the fact that it did have his name on it. If he had just one legitimate business, this was probably it. I wondered if this might have been the sight of my beating. As I thought back on it, it had had the feel of a back room of a bar.

I had followed Meredith Hannigan to the bar. She had parked at the curb and entered while I had wrestled with the decision whether or not to follow her in. I didn't have a plan for what I would do once I was in there. But it would probably be my best chance to get definitive proof that she was The Woodstock Baby, or not, in which case I would be back to square one. I decided to go for it.

I pulled the solid wood door open. It was heavy, like a bulwark. It felt like entering the dragon's den. It was dim, cool and quiet, and felt menacing, although that might have just been me. For other people it might have felt warm and welcoming, but somehow I doubted that. It did indeed look like a den. A long bar ran along the left wall. Liquor bottles lined the wall behind the bar like chess pieces ready for battle. Along the right wall were booths, the seats of which were stitched maroon leather topped by those little brass tacks, just like the chairs that used to be in my grandpa's den.

Meredith Hannigan sat on a barstool, one long leg crossed over the other. She looked very comfortable as she turned her head and looked at me. She smiled and said, "I wondered if you were going to come in."

That took me by surprise. "You, uh, what?" I stammered.

"You've been following me," she said, "so I wondered if you would follow me in here."

"Oh," I said.

Meredith patted the stool next to hers. "Have a seat."

This definitely wouldn't have been part of the plan, even if I had had one, but I was nothing if not flexible. I walked to her side. My brain hadn't caught up with my legs yet. I slid onto the stool next to her's. "Hi," I said, and then immediately felt like an idiot.

Meredith laughed. She had a throaty, sophisticated laugh. "What are you drinking?"

"What are you drinking?" I said, nodding at the glass in front of her.

"Iced tea."

"That'll work," I said.

"Will," she said to the bartender. "Set my friend up."

Will the Bartender was at least sixty. He wore black pants and a white shirt with black suspenders. I would have bet that his socks were white. He moved at glacier speed to the end of the bar and filled a glass with ice and then poured tea from a picture.

"What's your name?" Meredith said while we watched Will.

"Chase," I said.

"First name or last?"

"Last."

"Okay, Mr. Chase," she said.

"Just Chase," I said.

Meredith nodded. Will made it back with the iced tea and set it in front of me.

Meredith held her glass in front of me. "Cheers."

I touched my glass to hers. "Cheers." When our glasses touched, the overhead lights glinted off the rim of Meredith's glass and reflects into her eyes. They sparkled in that glint of light. Until that moment I hadn't noticed, but now I saw that she had the same silvery, gray eyes as Caroline Wolf.

Meredith sipped some tea through the straw in her glass, and then set it down on the bar. "So why are you following me?"

When I had entered the bar I had hoped to find something that would prove that Meredith Hannigan was the daughter that Caroline Wolf had given birth to at Woodstock. I had tons of circumstantial evidence and now the eyes. There was a chance it was just a coincidence, but combined with all the other evidence, I was sure.

I took a drink of the iced tea to stall while I made up my mind. "Okay," I said, "I'm just going to lay it out there. This will probably be hard for you to hear, but I don't know any other way to say it."

"Hey!"

I turned my attention from Meredith to the back of the bar where the "Hey" had come from. Will the Bartender was standing next to an irate-looking fire plug of a man. He was about 5'6" with a barrel chest and thick stubby arms covered in a mass of curly gray hair, which also sprouted from the v-neck of his tee shirt. His head was covered by a thin sheen of gray hair and his face was beet red under a solid white goatee.

"I thought I told you not to come back here," he said, pointing a thick stubby finger at me.

I looked behind me and then back at the irate man. "Are you talking to me?"

He strode across the plank floor and poked me in the chest with the stubby sausage link shaped finger. "Yeah, I'm talking to you."

"What the hell, Frank?" Meredith said.

"Stay out of this, Meredith," Frank said.

I brought my hand up to swat the finger away. Frank must have leaned in because the back of my hand connected with his lantern jaw. He was momentarily stunned, and then reached in and grabbed two fists full of my shirt and hoisted me off the bar stool.

"You didn't get enough the last time?"

And then it hit me. This was the guy who had put the beating on me before. I was taken aback. I had gotten my ass kicked by a five and a half foot tall senior citizen. The guys at O'Ryan's would never let me live that down. I looped both hands around his arms and boxed his ears with the palms of my hands. He staggered back and the grip on my shirt loosened enough that I was able to shove him off of me. As far as I was concerned it was over, but I stepped back and readied myself for more if Frank was so inclined. Then Will the Bartender whacked me across the back with a chair. They don't break like they do in the movies. The skinny old man didn't have much force, but it was enough to knock the wind out of me and drive me to one knee. I was just about to stand up when the bulwark door swung open and a whole platoon of blue shirted cops ran in and piled on top of me.

CHAPTER THIRTY-FIVE

I was dragged out of the dog pile, cuffed, and thrown in the back of a patrol car. It was my first time in the back of a police car, and it took less than a minute to figure out I didn't like it. After that realization, I realized that Ford was driving the car.

"Hey Ford," I said. "What the hell?"

"What the hell, what?" Ford said.

"What the hell am I being arrested for?"

"For assaulting Frank Hannigan."

"He started it," I said.

Ford laughed and looked at me in the rearview mirror. "Is that the defense you're going to go with?"

Then I made my most important realization. "Wait a minute. Frank Hannigan? As in Captain Hannigan?"

"Yep."

"Ah shit," I said.

"Yep," Ford said. "You screwed the pooch."

"Shit," I said again. I thought about asking Ford to get me out of there, but the kid was already in too deep. So I rode the rest of the way in silence, cursing my bad luck.

I was fingerprinted, which was actually pretty cool because they utilized a digital fingerprinting system. I put my fingers on a plate of glass and my prints were scanned into the computer system. As far as I knew, the Detroit Police were still using ink pads and paper. I was then photographed and thrown into a holding cell.

I spent the night in the holding cell. I was given a bologna sandwich for dinner, but that was the extent of the hospitality. I didn't even get a blanket or pillow. I was doing hard time. I dreamt of being in Andy Griffith's jail with Otis the drunk and Aunt Bea's fried chicken.

I woke the next morning thinking that I had been forgotten, but after a couple of hours of sitting there and thinking about what I had done, I was taken from the cell, in handcuffs, and driven across town to a small, square brick courthouse.

I had no idea what to expect, but I was pleasantly surprised to find Sarge sitting in the courtroom. I was even more pleased to see Assistant Prosecutor Julie Runyon standing at the prosecution table when my name was called and I was led into the courtroom.

I stood at the defense table in cuffs, unsure what to do. The court reporter read the charges. I was surprised to hear that I was being charged with aggravated assault.

"Where's your lawyer?" the judge said.

His voice was high and squeaky and even though he sat behind the big bench it was obvious that he was a little man. His features were small and delicate and he had a nervous way about him, like a Chihuahua. His grayish black hair was combed over the top of his bald head. He wore small round glasses and a polka dot bow tie. A brass plate attached to the front of the bench said Honorable Arthur P. Evans.

I looked around. Nobody came to my rescue. "I guess I don't have one," I said.

"Well, I guess you don't need one for this, but get one before you come in here again."

"Yes, sir," I said.

"How do you plead?"

"Not guilty."

"Where do we stand on bail, Miss Runyan?" the judge said.

"The prosecution does not oppose a PR bond, Your Honor."

"Personal Recognizance?" the judge said, flabbergasted. "This man assaulted a prominent member of our community."

"Allegedly, Your Honor," Julie Runyon said.

"Yeah, yeah," the judge said. "I am not inclined to let someone accused of such a crime out without bail."

Sarge stood up and said, "Your Honor. I am Mr. Chase's business partner and we worked together for more than 15 years on the Detroit Police force. I am confident that he will appear and am more than willing to put my bar up to ensure his appearance at court."

The judge looked irritated. "That's fine," he said. "That's a conversation you can have with a bail bondsman, now sit down."

"Oh, sure," Sarge said. He slowly sat back down.

"Bail set at $100,000," the judge said. He banged his gavel and I was taken back to my cell.

I sat in the cell for another couple hours until Ford appeared at the door with a key. "You made bail," he said, unlocking the door. I followed him back to the lobby of the police station to find Sarge standing there with a rat.

He wasn't really a rat, but he looked like one. Bennie Bales was no more than five three and probably didn't weigh a hundred pounds. He had pasty skin, pointy ears and a pointy nose. His black hair was slicked back revealing an exaggerated widow's peak. He wore black jeans and a black leather sport coat over a black silk shirt open at the collar. He looked like Joe Peschi in the movie My Cousin Vinny.

"You gotta be shittin' me," I said.

"You wanna go back inside?" Bennie said. "Be my guest."

"Not here," Sarge said. "Let's take it outside."

Bennie Bales was the bail bondsman in the office next to O'Ryan's. I never knew if Bales was his real name or if he changed it to go along with the bail bondsman thing. He was an arrogant little prick with a chip on his shoulder the size of Mt. Rushmore. His mouth never stopped running, writing checks he couldn't cash. But I never heard of anybody actually trying to cash one. It would have been like beating up someone's little brother.

I followed Sarge and Bennie out into the parking lot. Bennie spun on my as soon as we hit the asphalt.

"Fuck you, Chase," he said. "I come all the way out to cow country to bail your ass out, and this is the thanks I get?"

I looked at Sarge.

"What?" Sarge said. "I don't know anybody around here. Besides he's doing us a favor."

"A favor?"

"He's posting the bail against the bar, and he's not taking a fee."

"Get out of here. Is there really a tiny little heart in there somewhere," I said, ruffling Bennie's oiled up hair.

"Get the fuck off a me," Bennie said. He lurched away from me, using both hands to slick his hair back into place. He then walked back to the giant black Cadillac he drove.

"Thanks, Bennie," I said.

Bennie threw one more Fuck you over his shoulder before climbing into the car and driving away.

I looked at Sarge. "How'd you pull that one off?"

Sarge smiled. "I told him you'd owe him a favor."

I sighed. "I think I'd rather be in jail."

Sarge laughed. He pulled a business card out of his shirt pocket and held it out to me. "That prosecutor girl told me to give you this."

I took the card from Sarge and looked at it. "Justin Bowyer, Esquire. What's this?"

"The prosecutor girl said you should call this guy. She said you need a lawyer."

CHAPTER THIRTY-SIX

There was a note stuck under the windshield of my car, asking me to stop in at the coffee shop where I had met with Art Pindar. I found Meredith Hannigan sitting at the same table, with the ceramic tile mosaic top, that I had sat at when I had met Art Pindar. She wore white capri pants, a blue sleeveless top, and sandals. A pair of sunglasses sat on the top of her head. She had some kind of a coffee shake in front of her, but she wasn't drinking it. I sat in the chair across from her.

"You said you had something to tell me that I wasn't going to want to hear."

"I did," I said, "right before your brother jumped me, and Will the Bartender whacked me with a chair."

"I'm really sorry about that," Meredith said. "I'm going to do what I can to get the charges dropped."

"Let me ask you something. Why do you think Frank jumped me?"

"I honestly have no idea," she said.

I looked into those silvery gray eyes and I believed her. I sighed.

"I'm helping out a very nice lady who is desperate to save her daughter's life. I can't even tell you the medical part. All I know is she needs a bone marrow transplant."

Meredith looked confused. "What does that have to do with me?"

I held up my index finger. "Hang on," I said, "we'll get to you."

She nodded. Her coffee shake thing was sweating and the moisture filled the cracks between the mosaic tiles.

"This nice lady went to Woodstock 44 years ago and had a baby."

"At the concert?"

I nodded.

"Is that the daughter that's sick?"

"No."

"Didn't they make a movie about a baby being born at Woodstock? Is that the one?"

She was really getting into the story.

"Yes, they did," I said. "But that's not the one. Let me go on with the story."

I told Meredith Hannigan about Caroline Wolf's trip to the most famous concert in history and the baby she had, and lost, there.

"You have to admit," she said, "that's a little far-fetched. He told her the baby died and he buried it and she believed him?"

"Yes and no. You have to remember, she was only 19. She had no idea what to do. Whether she actually believed it or not, she chose to believe it."

Meredith's face said she didn't like it, but she said, "Okay. So what does this have to do with me."

"Well," I said, "this nice old lady asked me to find that baby. She hopes that that person will be a match for her sick daughter and will be willing to help save her life."

"I thought the baby was dead?"

"She chose to believe it, at the time. Now she hopes she was wrong. I came here because the father of the baby, the guy who said it was dead, lived here."

"And you thought you could get the truth out of him?"

"That was the plan."

"Was?"

I nodded. "He was killed a long time ago, so I didn't get much from him. However, I am an experienced investigator, and I asked around."

"And?"

"And I believe that the baby is still alive. I have a witness that saw a young man walking away from the concert with a baby wrapped in a towel."

"That doesn't mean that it was the same baby."

108

"The young man she described sounded a lot like your brother Michael."

That got hcr. "What?" she said breathlessly.

"I also discovered that some of the young men in this town gave your father things in exchange for deferments from the war. And I believe the baby's father was one of them."

"Wait a minute. You're telling me this guy gave my father a baby?"

"Yes."

"And what did my father do with this baby?"

I didn't want to say it. I had hoped she would figure it out for herself. "I believe he switched it with his baby, the one that was so sick. The one that everyone thinks was saved by a miracle."

Meredith gave me the deer in the headlights look. It took her a few seconds to process what I had said. "You think *I'm* the baby?" she said, placing her hand on her chest.

I nodded.

"Well, you're wrong."

"I have a witness that—"

"You're wrong," she again, firmer. She pushed back from the table hard enough to knock the chair over, and stormed out of the coffee shop.

I remained seated at the table with the coffee shake thing. It was melting. I sighed. This case was wearing me out. "I told you you weren't going to want to hear it," I said. It gave me no comfort to have been right.

I wondered if I had gone too far. I decided that I hadn't. I couldn't think of any other way I could have told her. It was like having a piano fall on you. It was going to hurt no matter how it happened.

The little bell that hung on the handle of the coffee shop door tinkled and I looked up. Meredith Hannigan walked in. She righted the chair and sat down opposite from me.

"I always felt like I was different from them," she said. "I mean look at me. I'm taller than my brothers and my father. I have fair skin and blond hair while they have olive skin and thick dark hair. My mom told me I was crazy. She said I was as much a Hannigan as any of them."

"She didn't know," I said.

Meredith nodded her head as if it confirmed something. "Good. This is bad enough without my mother being a part of it." She blew out a breath. "Are you sure?"

I nodded. "Pretty sure."

"How do we find out for sure?"

"I'm sure you've seen one of these on TV," I said, holding up a long tube with a long Q-Tip inside it. "Run the Q-Tip along the inside of your cheek and put it back into the tube. I'll take it to the doctors and they'll run DNA on it, and compare it to the nice lady I was telling you about. They'll also compare it to her daughter to see if you are a match to be a donor."

Meredith reached across the table and took the tube from my hand. She uncorked it and removed the Q-Tip. She hesitated for a moment and then stuck it in her mouth and rubbed it around the inside of her cheek. She then stuck it back in the tube, re-corked it, and handed it back to me.

"Do you want to know about them?" I asked.

"No," she said. "Let's wait and see what the tests say."

CHAPTER THIRTY-SEVEN

I have to admit, I was pretty pleased with myself when I got back to O'Ryan's. I had no idea how long it would take to get the DNA results back on the swab I had taken from Meredith Hannigan, but I was almost 100% certain that she was The Woodstock Baby. I just hoped that she was a match for Sarah Wolf, and would be willing to donate bone marrow to her long lost sister. I'd hate to have stirred everything up and then not have it work out.

I sat at the bar with my hand wrapped around a cold beer. The Tigers were on the TV over the bar, leading the Minnesota Twins 3 to 1 with 2 outs in the top of the sixth. Verlander struck out Mauer with a nasty curve ball to end the inning and the broadcast went to commercial.

A couple of the regulars came in and climbed onto stools next to mine. Officers Hendrix and Sullivan were partners in a patrol car. As Hendrix was black and Sullivan was white, they had acquired the obvious nickname, Salt and Pepper.

They couldn't have been more different. Sullivan was a downriver hillbilly. He wore a flannel shirt with the sleeves cut off and a pair of frayed blue jeans. His arms looked like pipe cleaners sticking out of the frayed holes. Hendrix wore a tank top with the Gold's Gym logo on the front. He looked like the guy in the logo, right down to the bald head and the bowling ball-sized biceps.

"Hey, Chase," Sullivan said. He flashed Sarge the peace sign.

Sarge understood that he was ordering two beers and not actually saying peace. He grabbed a couple long necks out of the cooler under the bar and slid them in front of Salt and Pepper.

"What's the score?" Hendrix asked.

"Three one, us," I said, "Bottom six."

"What'd Torii do?"

I let him stew for a couple seconds and then said, "Two run homer in the first."

"My man," Hendrix said, extending his fist. I bumped knuckles with him and he did the explosion thing. I laughed.

"Hey, Chase," Sullivan said.

"You already said that," I said.

"You hear about the cop got hit by a car," he continued as if I hadn't spoken.

It sounded like the setup to a joke. "No, what about the cop got hit by a car." I smiled, waiting for the punch line.

"It's not a joke," Sullivan said. "Some poor sap in a town west of here. He was standing on the side of the road next to a car he had pulled over. Some son of a bitch side-swiped him."

"What was the name of the town?" I said, dread filling my stomach.

"I don't remember," Sullivan said.

"Saline," Hendrix said. "I remember cause it's like the stuff I use on my contacts."

I groaned. "What was the cop's name?"

"That one I remember," Sullivan said.

"Everybody in this town knows that name," Hendrix said.

"Ford," I sighed.

CHAPTER THIRTY-EIGHT

"You've got to be kidding me," I said to myself, looking at the blood stain on the road. I couldn't believe they couldn't have come up with something original. Or were they trying to send a message of some sort?

Unfortunately, for them, they underestimated Ford. Hitting a guy the size of an F250 with a car wasn't enough. Sure they had messed him up pretty good, but they hadn't killed him. If they were trying to silence him, or me, they failed.

The hospital was swarming with cops, waiting for their comrade to come out of surgery, so I had avoided going there. Besides, I wasn't going to get much from him while he was unconscious on an operating table.

The TV news had confirmed what Salt and Pepper had told me, Ford had a car pulled over when another car sideswiped him, pinning him between the car he had pulled over and the car that had hit him. The driver had sped off after doing the deed. The teenager that Ford had pulled over for speeding was so shaken up she had been unable to tell police anything about the hit and run driver. It looked like finding the driver would be all but impossible, which is exactly what they wanted. Unless Ford pulled through.

I was angry. I felt responsible for the blood on the road. I had let the kid blunder around in a murder investigation he had no business messing with. He was in the hospital because I didn't protect him.

As I stood on the side of the road kicking myself, my cell phone vibrated in my pocket. I pulled it out and looked at the screen. It said restricted. I flipped open the phone anyway and answered.

"Is this Chase?" the caller said.

"It is," I said.

"Joe Walsh is the key to solving this."

I pulled the phone away from my ear and looked at it. It didn't tell me anything. I put it back to my ear and said, "Who is this," but the line was dead. The mystery caller was gone.

I closed the phone and put it back in my pocket. "Joe Walsh?" I said to myself. "From The Eagles?"

I tried to put Joe Walsh out of my mind and went to see Aunt Jenny again. My last visit had been a tea party, this one wasn't. Aunt Jenny seemed irritated and it came off as hostile towards me.

"What is it, Mr. Chase?" she said.

"I want to talk to you about Peter Wilson," I said.

"Am I missing something? Didn't we already have this talk?"

"Yes, we did. But some new developments have come up."

"New developments? It was 40 years ago."

"Yes, it was," I conceded.

"Then what new could there be?"

"Officer Ford was hit by a car yesterday."

"I heard," she said, "but what does that have to do with Peter?"

"You don't think it's a coincidence? Ford getting hit by a car?"

"I do think it's a coincidence. That's all it is."

"It's a little too coincidental," I said. "Getting hit by a car seems to be the way they get rid of people around here."

"What are you talking about? Peter hitting that man was an accident, and I have to believe that Officer Ford's accident was nothing more than an accident as well."

"Unless you look at it like this: I have a witness that says Peter admitted to doing 'something horrible' to get out of going to Vietnam. It was eating him up. Officer Ford was looking into it. He didn't believe that it was an accident. And now he's been hit and almost killed."

114

Aunt Jenny took a big breath and let it out slowly. Her demeanor changed.

"You know more than you're saying," I said.

She nodded her head. If I didn't know better I would have sworn she was holding back tears.

"What is it?"

"He told me," she said.

I felt a surge of adrenaline. "Told you what?"

"You're right that he wasn't dealing well with it. He was a mess. He told me that he ran Randy down on purpose. That it was the only way The Captain would give him a deferment."

"Son of a bitch," I said. I had pretty much figured it out, but never thought I'd be able to prove it. "Did he know why The Captain wanted Randy dead?"

"No, he didn't."

It didn't matter, I knew why.

CHAPTER THIRTY-NINE

I was back at O'Ryan's, sitting at the bar with my hand wrapped around a cold beer. I couldn't think of anything more to do until Ford was able to talk.

"Joe Walsh?" Sarge said. "Why does that name sound familiar?"

"He played in The Eagles."

"Linebacker, right?"

"Not the Philadelphia Eagles," I said. "The rock band The Eagles."

"Oh," Sarge said. Then he got a confused look on his face. "Why would this mystery caller want you to talk to a musician?"

"I don't know."

"Did this band play at Woodstock?"

"I don't think so."

Sally had been listening to our conversation from the other end of the bar. She wandered down to our end and said, "Do you two law enforcement professionals think there could be another Joe Walsh besides the guy from The Eagles?"

I looked at Sally and then back at Sarge with my eyebrows raised.

"I guess it's possible," Sarge said. "Joe is a pretty common name."

I looked back at Sally. "Do you think you could look him up on that internet thing of yours?"

Sally said, "If I didn't know better I'd swear you two morons set me up."

She went through the swinging door to the back room. Sarge was concentrating on a crossword puzzle. I drank my beer and tried to figure out how to connect The Captain to the two murders.

"I found Joe Walsh," Sally said, returning from the back room.

"Cool," I said.

"Well, sort of," she said.

"What does 'sort of' mean?"

"He's dead."

"That's going to make it hard for me to interview him, Sally."

"I know."

"He wasn't hit by a car, was he?"

"No. He was killed in 1966. In Vietnam."

I sighed, very frustrated.

"Why would someone tell me to talk to Joe Walsh? Am I supposed to go see a psychic? Or maybe that kid from that movie that saw dead people?"

"I loved that movie," Sarge said. "I never guessed the ending.

"I thought you said the caller said Joe Walsh was the key that would help you?" Sally said, ignoring her uncle.

"Yeah, something like that," I said.

"Right," Sally said. "So, I dug a little further and found that Joe Walsh's father, Andrew, was the police chief in Saline in the sixties and seventies."

"Well I'll be," I said. "Do you know where I can find him?"

"Of course I do," Sally said with a mocking tone.

"Would you mind sharing?"

Sally laughed and told me where I could find the retired police chief.

Now the question was, could I get him to talk?

CHAPTER FORTY

Ford had made it through surgery and had been transferred to a regular room in the small hospital. From what I had been able to get from one of the floor nurses, his right femur had been crushed and the doctors had had to graft bone into what was left of it, and put in a steel rod that would be a part of Ford for the rest of his life. The rest of the police department had left the hospital when he had been brought out of surgery and they were pretty sure he would survive. I had taken the opportunity to sneak in to see him.

I sat at his bedside watching him sleep, trying to figure out how my seemingly simple pseudo-missing persons case had morphed into murder, and a hit and run on a police officer. It was not what I had expected when I had first entered this idyllic town.

There was no doubt in my mind that this accident had not been an accident. Whoever had hit Ford had meant to do it. The only question that remained was if they had been sending some kind of message to back off, or if they had intended to kill him and had messed up.

The door to the room opened and I stiffened, preparing myself for a confrontation with a member of the Saline Police, or one of The Captain's goons. The man who entered was neither. He was an older and, although it seemed impossible, bigger version of Officer Ford. He had the same blunt cut hair and a weathered face that had seen several decades of outdoor activity. He wore blue jeans and work boots and a short-sleeved button up checked shirt. Huge, powerful hands held a ball cap by the visor, crushing and twisting it.

He looked shocked to see me. "Who are you?" he said. His voice was deep and rumbled softly.

I stood up and extended my hand over the hospital bed that separated us. "My name is Chase," I said.

The big man eyed me up and down and shook my hand. His grip was that of a man who had learned to temper it so as not to crush every hand he shook.

"Is there a problem?" I said, feeling his gaze weigh heavy on me.

"No, no problem. I just expected more, the way my son went on about you. He talked as if you were some kind of superhero or something."

I smiled. "I'm no superhero."

"I can see that," the elder Ford said.

I laughed and then said, "I'm really sorry about this," nodding my head at the man's son lying in the hospital bed.

He sighed and slumped into the chair on the other side of his son's bed. "Ain't your fault. It's this goddamn town. I'd a left long ago if it weren't for the farm. It's about all we got. I wouldn't know what to do to support my family without it. So I have to stay."

I nodded. "So what happened here?"

"I don't know. All they tell me is that it was a hit and run and they're working on it."

"Do you believe that?"

"What? That they're working on it?"

"Yeah."

The big man looked at his son. It was probably the same look he used when his boy was a baby, sleeping in his crib. "I'd like to think they're working on it."

"But you don't believe it."

"I know Jimmy was looking into some things that were probably ruffling some feathers. I told him to leave it be but he wouldn't listen. He can be stubborn."

I smiled. I knew the type. They made for good cops. "You think they were trying to shut him down?"

"That's what they do. Kind of like damage control. They'll probably come for you next."

CHAPTER FORTY-ONE

"You know you're fucked, right?"

I was sitting across a desk from Justin Bowyer, Esquire. He was a white kid with a blonde afro. His cheeks were smooth and rosy. He wore a short sleeved white dress shirt with more wrinkles than Betty White's ass, and a polyester tie with a huge knot that hung loose below his chin.

"Because I have a 12 year old for a lawyer?" I said.

"Wow, good one," Bowyer said. "I've never heard that one." He pointed above and behind his head without taking his eyes off me. "You see that?"

How could I miss it? It was a diploma from the University of Michigan Law School approximately the size of a billboard. If it was any bigger Bowyer would need a bigger office.

Bowyer head up his index finger. "First in my class," he said.

"Is the ink dry?"

Bowyer was getting irritated. "You don't have to be here," he said. "You think I don't have people lined up outside my door, wanting me to represent them?"

I didn't recall seeing anyone lined up outside the door, but held up my hand and said, "Okay, don't get all worked up. Tell me, why am I fucked?"

"Because you assaulted a Hannigan in Saline."

"He started it," I said.

"Now who's the 12 year old? The Captain has that whole damn town under his thumb. The police chief and the mayor are his kids and Judge Evans has been in his pocket since before I was born. There is no way you're going to get the case dropped, or win it. You will lose and you will go to prison. In other words—"

"I'm fucked."

Justin Bowyer, Esquire nodded his head in triumph. "I couldn't have said it better myself."

"The fat lady's not singing yet," I said.

"She's warming up."

"Well, I guess I'll just have to get them before they get me."

CHAPTER FORTY-TWO

I entered O'Ryan's to the typical mid-week scene. The Tigers played on the TV above the bar – a quick check told me they were in Kansas City, and losing. That was nothing new. The Tigers always struggled with the Royals. Why was one of life's many mysteries. A few of the cops sat at the bar and watched the game. Most sat at tables swapping stories of their night.

Out of the corner of my eye I saw Caroline Wolf sitting alone in a booth along the back wall. She was slumped over holding her head in her hands. A short glass half full of amber liquid sat centered below her chin on the table.

"How long has she been here?" I asked Sarge.

"Hour or so," Sarge said.

"How many has she had?"

"That's the first one."

I threaded my way through the tables and slid in the booth across from Caroline Wolf. "Come here often?" I said.

She raised her head and looked at me. The sorrow that filled her eyes made me conclude that her daughter Sara had died.

"The DNA came back," she said. "Meredith Hannigan is my daughter."

"Oh," I said. "Well, that's good, right? So why the long face?"

"What do I say to her? How do I explain to her how I let her be taken from me...and did nothing about it?"

"There were extenuating circumstances," I said.

"Oh, bullshit. I allowed it to happen. I did nothing to try and find her. I'm a terrible excuse for a human being."

I paused for a moment and then said, "I don't know what to tell you. I do know that Meredith was raised in a good home with a loving, doting mother. She has done very well for herself and I don't think she holds any ill will towards you."

"You don't think."

I nodded. "I honestly don't know for sure, but if you want I'll go with you to meet her."

Caroline Wolf nodded and picked up her glass. She took a tiny sip, and set it back on the table with a grimace. "This stuff is awful."

I smiled. "Yeah, well, I don't know if you've noticed, but this ain't exactly The Whitney."

CHAPTER FORTY-THREE

Like everybody else involved in this case, Andrew Walsh was old. He was really old, but didn't look it. He stood tall and straight, a shade over six feet and skinny as a rail. He wore plaid dress pants in different shades of gray and a blue button-up short sleeved shirt. His shoes were shined and he wore a thin gold wedding ring.

He had agreed to meet with me, but said he had a doctor's appointment. As it turned out, he needed a ride, so I told him to save the cab fare and I'd take him. I picked him up from the apartment complex where he lived and we chatted about our police careers while we drove to the doctor's office.

I sat in the waiting room and entertained myself perusing a stack of magazines about Detroit. If I didn't know better, I'd think Detroit was a pretty nice place, based on the articles in the magazines. Unfortunately, I did know better. The Detroit portrayed in the magazines was not the Detroit I had worked and lived in.

After what seemed like hours, Walsh finally returned from the back of the doctor's office. "Everything good?" I asked.

"Fit as a fiddle and ready to dance," he said, and actually did a little two step.

I laughed and escorted the old man out of the office and back into the car. We drove through McDonald's and got two cups of coffee, and then I turned the conversation back to 1969.

"Tell me about The Captain," I said.

Walsh's mood darkened. "What's to tell?"

"There's a lot to tell," I said and told him everything I knew.

We drove aimlessly around the town while I told my story. Walsh said nothing. He stared out the windshield and listened. I wondered how much of what I was telling him he already knew. By the time I finished my story we were pulling into Oakwood Cemetery. I followed the one lane road as it wound through countless tombstones and came to a stop next to one I had found before I had picked up Andrew Walsh.

A simple brown plaque was attached to a low gray headstone. It was angled so that we could read it from the car. Raised gold letters said:

Joseph A. Walsh
PFC US Army
Vietnam
OCT 26 1947 APR 11 1966

"I received an anonymous call," I said. "The caller told me that Joe Walsh was the key to solving my case. Do you know why that would be?"

Walsh stared out the passenger window at his son's grave marker and then slowly opened the door and climbed from the car. He walked hesitantly to the grave and stopped short, as if not wanting to stand on his son.

I exited the car and followed the old man. I stood silently, waiting for him to speak.

"Joe was drafted," he finally said. "He wasn't thrilled by it, but he wasn't scared to go. It was his duty, he said. He was a good soldier from what I heard. One of his buddies came and visited me when he got back. He told me about Joe's death.

"He was about half way through his tour when his unit was sent to Xa Cam My on a search and destroy mission. It was Easter Sunday April 10, 1966. They were there to lure out a Viet Cong battalion. They did, and got a battle nobody expected.

"Joe's company got separated from the other two that were there and they stumbled upon the battalion. They were outnumbered more than two to one and took heavy casualties, Joe being one of them."

"I'm sorry," I said, and I really was. It had been almost 50 years since his son had died, but the pain that radiated from Andrew Walsh was profound. I was sure he would take it to the grave, just like Evelyn Wilson. There was too much pain in this damn town.

He looked at me as if he had forgotten that I was there then went back to looking at his son's grave. His voice hardened as he said, "I had two other boys and I was not going to lose them too. John was a senior in high school. His dream was to be a cop, like his old man. I was determined to keep him out of that war.

"I went to The Captain. He was the head of the local draft board, but he was also a business man. He was running that bar of his, but he was also running prostitutes."

"He was?" I hadn't seen that coming.

The old man nodded. "Back in the old days, before even my time, there was a hotel in the building where The Captain's bar is. It hadn't been used as a hotel in years, but the rooms were still there. The Captain had his girls up there. His customers would set up a date with the bartender who would then send the men up.

"I wasn't the chief yet, but I knew what was going on. Hell, most everybody who cared to know knew what was going on. So I went to The Captain and threatened to bust him if he didn't give John a deferment."

Walsh turned his head and looked at me. The look dared me to say something negative to him. I didn't.

"Yes, Mr. Chase," Walsh said, reading my mind, "it was me. I was the one that got The Captain started. I was the one who put the idea into his head that he could trade deferments for stuff. And he did.

"A couple of years later I became the chief. Yes, The Captain owned me. He did pretty much whatever he wanted in this town and I didn't see, hear, or know anything about it. But, John, and my other boy, Robert, stayed out of Vietnam and are still alive today, so I don't give a damn what anyone thinks or says about me. I did what I did, and I'd do it again."

"Do you know anything about his daughter? About her birth or 'miracle recovery'?"

Walsh shook his head slowly. "Like I just said, I didn't see, hear, or know anything about The Captain."

I took Walsh back to the retirement home where he lived. Unlike Agnes Adams's home, the residents weren't locked in, and there wasn't an airlock to enter through.

He led me through a day room where residents were watching The Price is Right. The volume was loud enough to run off every rodent in the building. The residents all had blank looks on their faces and I was reminded of a saying I had heard once – "Inside every old person is a young person who wonders what happened."

Walsh led me to the dining room. It was easily the gaudiest dining hall I had ever been in. It looked like a casino with dinner tables rather than blackjack tables. The same garish, wildly patterned carpet that existed in every casino in the world covered the floor. The chairs were upholstered in a clashing, yet equally offensive pattern. The valances over the windows matched the chairs. The clanging of pots and pans and the smell wafting from the kitchen told me that lunch was drawing near. Walsh sat at a table for four, already set for lunch. I sat in the chair next to his.

I hoped that his confession about blackmailing The Captain wasn't an aberration, but an opening of the flood gates. I didn't beat around the bush. We were both cops in another lifetime. There was no need to waste time, and with lunch drawing nigh, I didn't want to be interrupted. "Tell me about the death of Randy Adams," I said.

Walsh looked off to the far corner of the dining room, but I knew he wasn't studying the hideous wall paper, he was looking back to 1970. "Randy Adams," he said, "was a known drug addict who was always stumbling around town, high on one thing or another. I'm sure he had family and some friends who were probably saddened by his death, but not surprised. By that time if he hadn't been hit by a car, he probably would have overdosed. It's my opinion that the car simply sped up the process."

"Was it an accident?"

"What else would it have been?" he said, bringing his eyes back to me.

"Murder?"

"Murder?" He seemed shocked by the thought.

"Murder," I said, nodding. "I'm pretty sure I know the motive, I just want your opinion. What happened back then? Did you investigate it as a murder?"

"We investigated, but we didn't get far enough to decide one way or the other about whether it was a murder."

"You stopped investigating?"

Walsh nodded.

"The Captain?"

Walsh nodded again. "He suggested that it would be better for everyone if we just put it down as an accident and closed the file. My youngest son, Robert, was a senior in high school that year."

I understood completely what that meant. He closed the file and Robert got a deferment.

"Did you keep the file that had been started?"

"Hell, I don't know," the old man said. "It might be in storage somewhere. There wasn't much to it anyway. Like I said, we didn't get far before The Captain shut us down."

"What about the Wilson kid?" I said. "Suicide?"

"We had a witness to that one. No investigation was required."

"You had a witness whose two sons got deferments."

"You have to understand something," Walsh said, "a deferment could have been taken away at any time. Once you sold your soul, he owned you."

People were starting to wander into the dining room for lunch. I stood and said, "How are your boys now?"

"They're good," Walsh said, nodding his head. "Real good."

"Glad to hear it," I said, patting him on the shoulder.

CHAPTER FORTY-FOUR

I found Meredith Hannigan in the real estate office where she worked. Being the mayor of a small town didn't pay much. Nowhere near what she needed to keep up the house I had followed her to. Hence, the real estate sales job.

The office was in the same strip mall where I had lunch my first day in Saline. Ironic that I was that close to her my first day in town and didn't even know it. The front window was plastered with information sheets on available properties. The inside was plain; cheap, industrial carpet in a muted beige and walls that were painted with just a hint of a pale green. Several desks, the likes of which could be purchased at any office supply store in America, faced each other in two rows, like opposing football teams' offensive and defense lines.

Meredith sat behind a desk near the front door, working on a laptop. She looked up when a tiny bell announced my arrival. All the color drained from her face and she took a deep breath.

"Hi," I said.

Meredith let the breath out and said hello.

"Do you want to meet her?"

The color drained from Meredith's face. "My…um…mother?"

I smiled. "I don't think you need to call her Mom."

Meredith laughed nervously.

"Her name is Caroline Wolf, and she is a very nice lady. She's out in my car and I think she's just as nervous as you are."

"I don't know what to say to her."

"Well then it's going to be a short conversation because she doesn't know what to say to you either."

Meredith was silent for a second. She then closed her eyes and took a deep breath. She blew it out and said, "Okay, let's do it," as if she were about to jump off a cliff.

I went and got Caroline Wolf from the car and brought her into the office. Meredith stood to meet us. She extended her hand like we were clients shopping for a house. Caroline Wolf took the hand and used it to pull Meredith into an awkward hug. I noticed just how much the two women looked alike, and wondered how I hadn't known immediately that Meredith was The Woodstock Baby. Some detective I was. I excused myself and stepped out into the heat.

CHAPTER FORTY-FIVE

Caroline Wolf came out of the office about 10 minutes later. She wiped tears from her eyes with a wadded up tissue.

"How'd it go?" I said.

"She wants to see you," she said, walking past me without breaking stride.

I watched her climb into the passenger seat of the Charger, and then reentered the real estate office. Meredith was still at her desk. She too wiped at tears with a tissue. I walked over to her desk and sat in the client chair.

"You wanted to see me?"

She looked at me as if she hadn't been aware of my approach. "Oh, yes," she said. She looked out the plate glass window that fronted the office. "She's wonderful."

"Yes, she is," I agreed.

"I can't help but wonder what my life would have been if I had spent it with her. Don't get me wrong, I loved my mother dearly and enjoyed my childhood here, but still…"

"I understand," I said. "Is that what you wanted to tell me?"

Meredith brought her eyes back to me. They had hardened. The tears had dried. "That son of a bitch took me from my real mother," she said.

I knew the son of a bitch she was referring to was The Captain. "Yes, but—"

She cut me off. "No. No buts. Yes, Caroline was young and not in any position to take care of a baby, but that wasn't his decision to make, dammit. Besides, he didn't do this for me, he did this for him."

I couldn't believe I was defending the man, but I said, "Believe it or not, he did it for your mother, I mean his—"

"I know who you mean. But he's not God. He doesn't get to decide who gets what, or who goes to war and who doesn't."

"You know about—"

"Yes, I know about it. Everybody knows about it."

"Ok," I said. "So what do you propose we do about it?"

"I want to take him down," Meredith said in a hiss.

I was taken aback by the venom in her voice. I couldn't believe she really wanted to punish the only man she had ever known as her father in such a way as to bring out this vengeance.

"Do you want to think about it first?"

Meredith shook her head. "I've thought about nothing else since I gave you that DNA sample."

"So how do we do it?" I said. I imagined that she didn't have an idea, that her anger was fueling this. I was surprised when she actually did have a lead for me.

"I went to school with a guy named Max Bennett. He told me once that he knew that The Captain had killed people."

"Did he elaborate? Tell you who, or how he knew this?"

"No. At the time I didn't believe him, didn't want to believe him, even though I knew deep down that The Captain was a bad man."

"Why would this Max Bennett tell you this?"

Meredith smiled an ironic, wry grin. "We were young. He wanted to be my boyfriend and I turned him down. He said something like, 'well I don't want to go with you anyway, your dad has people killed.'"

"So, it could have been just rhetoric to save face."

Meredith shook her head. "I don't think so. The look on his face said he knew he was telling the truth. And as I said, I knew he was telling the truth. I just didn't want to believe it."

I nodded. "So, do you know where this Max is?"

"Not really. His parents are still in town, but I haven't seen Max in years."

"Okay," I said, standing up. "I'll find him."

CHAPTER FORTY-SIX

The first step in finding Max Bennett was to call Sally, which I did as soon as Caroline Wolf was safely back at the hospital.

"Can you do me a favor?" I said when Sally answered the phone at O'Ryan's.

"You're going to have to put me on the payroll if you keep asking for 'favors'," she said.

"You are on the payroll," I said.

"I'm on O'Ryan's payroll, not Magnum PI's."

I knew she was just busting my balls. "Anyway," I said, drawing it out to indicate that it was time to move on, "can you do one of those internet search things that you do?"

Sally chuckled. "Anything for you, Chase."

"That's what I like to hear. I'm looking for a guy named Max Bennett. About our age—"

"I'm a little younger than you, Dear."

I sighed. "Okay, about my age. Grew up here in Saline. I'd guess he—"

"Got him."

"What?"

"Max Bennett. Still lives there in Saline. Divorced. He's a teacher. From the look of the sweat suit I'd say a gym teacher, probably elementary school but that's just a guess."

I paused in disbelief at the speed in which she had found Bennett. In the silence I could hear Sally tapping away at the keys of her computer the way a concert pianist plays his instrument. I wanted to ask her how she had found him so fast but decided it would only open me up to snide remarks about my age and/or lack of technological skills.

"You want his home address?" Sally said. "I'll text it to you."

"Um, sure," I said, "that'd be great."

"Okay. It's on the way. Good luck."

The phone beeped in my ear and I pulled it away to look at the screen. Sure enough, it said I had a text message from Sally.

The address was a small ranch house about the size of a shoe box on a street lined with similar shoe box houses. I parked at the curb in front of a front yard proportionally sized to the house. The grass was a vibrant green that belied the heat wave. Bennett must have doused it with gallons of water every day.

I smelled the pleasant aroma of a barbecue grill wafting in the air and saw tendrils of smoke rising from behind the small house. I followed my nose up the driveway to the rear of the house. The back yard was ringed with a chain link fence. The grill sat on a cement pad patio, manned by a tall guy wearing flip-flops and an apron that said "Grill Master." He held a long handled spatula in one hand and a bottle of beer in the other. A teenage girl rocked slowly on one of those free-standing glider swings with the canopy top. She had ear buds in and was totally engrossed in her cell phone.

"Excuse me," I said.

The grill master looked at me. The big toothy grin that had been on his face dimmed when he realized he didn't know me. "Can I help you?" he said.

"I'm looking for Max Bennett," I said. "Is that you?"

"Sure is. What can I do for you?"

I stayed outside the fenced in backyard, giving Bennett a feeling of security. "My name is Chase," I said. "I wonder if I can ask you a couple questions?"

"About?"

"Meredith Hannigan. Specifically, something you said to Meredith Hannigan in seventh grade."

"What?" Bennett said, confused. He looked at the teenage girl. She hadn't even noticed my arrival, let alone heard anything I had said. Bennett turned back to me. "What are you talking about?"

I smiled, trying to lessen the tension that had enveloped Bennett. "Do you have another one of those?" I said nodding to the beer he held.

He looked down at the beer clutched in his hand as if he had forgotten he held it. "Oh, uh, sure." He whistled at the teenage girl to get her attention. She looked up, annoyed, and yanked one of the ear buds out. "Go get another beer, would ya, please?" Bennett said. The girl pushed herself up like she had a 500 pound barbell across her shoulders and entered the house through the sliding glass door.

While she was gone Bennett tended to the meat on the grill, maybe hoping that I would go away if he ignored me.

The girl returned with the beer and bumped it into Bennett's shoulder without looking up from the cell phone. He turned and accepted it. "Thanks, Honey," he said. "Why don't you…" He stopped when he realized that she couldn't hear him and whistled again. The girl stopped and again removed the ear bud. "Why don't you go inside until dinner is ready?"

For the first time the girl looked at me. She shrugged her shoulders and went back through the sliding door.

Bennett watched her go and then turned to me. "So, Meredith Hannigan."

I accepted the beer while still leaning on the outside of the fence. "Yep."

"You know who her dad is?"

"The Captain, yes. I hear he kills people."

"Who told you that?"

"You did, by way of Meredith Hannigan."

"Meredith told you I said that?"

"She did."

"Why would I believe that Meredith Hannigan told you that I told her that The Captain killed people?"

"You want to ask her?" I said, holding out my cell phone, cued up to Meredith's number.

Bennett looked at me and decided to call my bluff. "Okay," he said.

I pushed the send button and held the phone out to Bennett. He put the spatula down and took the phone. I could hear it ringing.

"Meredith?" he said. "No, it's Max Bennett." He stood a little straighter when he said it, and sucked in his stomach a little. "Okay. Okay. Are you sure?" Bennett turned his back to me. "I don't want any trouble. Okay. Okay. I will."

I leaned against the fence, drinking my beer, when he turned back to me and handed me the phone. "I was just a kid," he said. "A girl I had liked hurt me, so I tried to hurt her back."

"By telling her that her dad killed people? Is that what you told all the girls that shot you down?"

"No," Bennett said, defeated.

"So why'd you tell Meredith that?"

"I overheard my dad say it to my mom."

"In what context?"

"They were arguing, about insurance of all things. My mom wanted to shop around and my dad refused. My mom didn't grow up here so she didn't understand. My dad tried to tell her that The Captain owned the insurance agency and they couldn't leave it. When she argued my dad told her that The Captain kills people."

"Is your dad still around?"

"No," Bennett said. "He's gone. Cancer."

Dammit, I thought. I had hoped this would be the lead that would close this case. "So you don't know if he knew this for a fact, or if he just generalizing?"

"I do know. He knew for a fact."

"He did? What did he know?"

Bennett looked toward the door his daughter had gone through. "You don't understand," he said.

"I understand there is a young man in the hospital—"

"Do you want me to join him? Or maybe my kid?"

"No," I said. "I want you to help me put these guys away so you don't have to live with this hanging over your head."

Bennett shook his head. "I wish it was that easy."

"I'm close, Mr. Bennett. I just need someone willing to help me. Unfortunately, what I know isn't proof. I wasn't there."

Bennett sighed. "He saw The Captain's son, Frank, push a kid named Peter Wilson in front of a truck."

"Frank Hannigan? You're sure?"

"That's what he told me. He was in town one night. I don't remember for what, picking up a pizza or something. Anyway, he was in his car and saw Frank and Peter Wilson talking on the sidewalk. He couldn't hear what they were talking about, but Frank was pretty animated. I don't know why, but my dad stayed there and watched. Maybe he thought he could help Peter or something if there was trouble. But before he could do anything, Frank had grabbed Peter by the shoulders and threw him out into Michigan Ave., right in front of a truck."

"What did your father do?"

"Got the hell out of there."

"He didn't tell anybody what he saw?"

"Who was he going to tell?"

"Yeah, you're right," I said. "There was nowhere he could have gone and not ended up in front of a truck himself."

"What are you going to do with this?" Bennett said.

"I don't know," I admitted. "I might need you to tell your story to some people."

"No way. I told Meredith I'd tell you what I know, but I will not put my family in danger. As far as I know, The Captain and Frank don't even know I exist, and I'd just as soon keep it that way."

"Okay," I said. "Let me see what I can do."

CHAPTER FORTY-SEVEN

I sat at a small table, in a room smaller than an interrogation room, in the Washtenaw County Courthouse. I was there with my lawyer, the afroed Justin Bowyer, Esquire, and my prosecutor, the lovely Julie Runyon. They were both bright eyed and bushy tailed and on the edge of their seats as I reported on my conversations with Max Bennett and Aunt Jenny.

"That's awesome," Justin said when I had finished.

"It's hearsay," Julie said.

I couldn't believe that I was having this conversation with these two kids. I'd have bet that their ages added together wouldn't have matched mine. I probably would have lost the bet, but I still would have made it.

"I know," I said. "I'm going to have to get someone directly involved to flip."

"Who?" Julie said.

"Well, we do have some peripheral players in this, but from what I can tell the three main actors are The Captain, and Frank and Michael Hannigan." I thought back to the conversation I had with Michael on the street in front of Meredith's house, and the way he had pled with me to go away and leave all this alone. "I think Michael is the weak link."

"What about The Captain?" Julie said. "He's like ninety. Wouldn't he fall on his sword to protect his sons?"

"What do you think Justin?" I said.

"I don't think so," he said. "Granted, most of what I heard growing up was probably exaggerated, but if the stories are half true then he wouldn't be above sacrificing his sons to protect himself."

"I agree," I said. "Besides, he's the one who ruined a lot of lives for his own greed. I want him to go down. Hard."

"Okay," Julie said. "Go get me a witness with first-hand knowledge of The Captain's complicity and I'll take it to Gerald."

I sat in my car, waiting for the air conditioning to get cold, while contemplating my next move. My cell phone vibrated in my pocket. I pulled it out and recognized Ford's number.

"Yeah," I said into the phone.

"Mr. Chase?" a deep voice rumbled. "This is Jim Ford. Jimmy's dad."

"Oh, yes, Mr. Ford." I felt a chill go down my spine that had nothing to do with the air conditioning. "Is everything okay? Is, uh, Jimmy okay?"

"Yes, he's doing fine. He's sleeping right now."

"Oh, good," I said, relieved. "What can I do for you?"

"Well, Jimmy asked me to give you a call. You see, the police chief stopped by a little earlier and told us that they didn't have anything to go on with the hit and run. Jimmy didn't say anything to the chief, but he told me that he remembered the name of the girl he had pulled over when he got hit. He doesn't have any recollection of the car that hit him, but the girl he had pulled over was named Leigh Hoffman."

"Leigh Hoffman. Got it. Thank you, Mr. Ford."

I was about to hang up when Ford continued.

"I don't mind telling you I'm mighty worried about Jimmy. I know he'll heal from this injury, but I'm afraid he's woken a bear that's not going to leave him alone until it shuts him up for good."

"I understand, Mr. Ford," I said. "I'm going to stop the bear. I promise."

"I'm going to hold you to that, Mr. Chase," Ford said.

CHAPTER FORTY-EIGHT

Leigh Hoffman lived with her parents in a house roughly the size of the Detroit Public Library. I drove up the drive that cut through about half an acre of perfectly manicured, perfectly green lawn to a four car garage. A new looking, bright red Ford Focus was parked in front of the last garage door. A nineties-era Camaro, with more rust than paint of the surface, sat right in the middle of the drive. I parked behind the Camaro and climbed out.

I followed a walkway lined with landscape rocks and flowers to a massive wood front door. I rang the bell and heard it chime in the house. When nobody answered I wandered around to the back of the house. A wooden privacy fence ringed the backyard. From around the side of it I could see a golf course. I lifted the latch that held the door to the privacy fence and pushed it open. I stuck my head through the opening and saw a backyard that matched the front. I saw a kidney-shaped in-ground pool with a rock formation in in the bend of the kidney. A waterfall rolled off the rocks into the pool. It was quite impressive, like something you'd see on HGTV or The Real Housewives of Wherever. A young, blonde-haired girl in a skimpy white bikini lounged on a lounge chair. She wore sunglasses tinted the same color bronze as her skin and wires ran from her ears, obviously connected to ear buds. To her left lounged a young man with tattoos decorating a shirtless, leanly muscled torso. He had a goatee and a five o'clock shadow and looked to be at least twenty. Between the two was a small, glass table on which two beers sweated in the heat.

"Hello," I called.

The girl didn't flinch, but the guy jumped like he'd been electrocuted. It took a second for him to realize that I wasn't the girl's father and to regain his composure. When he was back under control, he poked the girl in the shoulder and pointed at me.

The girl looked at me for maybe half a second, and then looked away. "My parents aren't here."

I said, "I'm looking for Leigh Hoffman," but she hadn't removed the ear buds and hadn't heard me. I asked the guy, "Is she Leigh?"

He nodded and I walked over to where they lounged. I grabbed a chair from a patio set and dragged it over, situating it very close to Leigh's lounge chair. I sat, facing Leigh's right ear. I noticed that the beers had disappeared from the table between the two young people. I reached over and plucked the ear bud from the ear nearest to me.

"I told you my parents aren't here," the girl said with disgust, still not looking at me.

"That's okay," I said, "I'm not here to talk to them. But we can call them if you think they'd be interested in what's going on here." I pulled my cellphone out of my pocket and prepared to dial, even though I had no idea what number to punch in.

"Leigh," the guy said a little too urgently. I knew that he wasn't supposed to be there. I had gambled that it would be the girl who didn't want her parents called, but I'd take what I could get.

"Fine," Leigh said petulantly, pulling the other ear bud out. "What do you want?"

"I'm investigating the hit and run of Officer Ford."

"Who?"

"The police officer who was hit by the car while he had you pulled over."

"I don't know what you're talking about."

"Yes, you do."

"Well I didn't see anything."

"You didn't see anything? It happened less than a foot away from your driver's side door."

"I was texting my friend Alyssa when it happened, so I wasn't paying attention."

I was incredulous. "You were texting your friend while you were pulled over by a police officer?"

"What?" she said. "It's not like I was texting while I was driving."

She had me there. "Is that what you told the police who came to the scene?"

"Yes."

"And what did the officer you talked to say?"

"He told me it was my lucky day and that I could go."

"Just like that? He let you leave?"

"Yes."

"Do you remember his name?"

"No."

"What did he look like?"

"I don't know. He was old."

"Short?"

"I guess."

Hannigan. I sat back and thought for a minute. I actually wasn't surprised that he let her go. If The Captain was involved, as I suspected, they wouldn't want any witnesses.

"Did you happen to see the car that hit Officer Ford?"

"Just the back end as it was driving away."

"Do you know what kind of car it was?"

"It was green."

"Green?"

"Or maybe blue."

"Maybe blue?"

"I don't know," Leigh said, perturbed that I was trying to pin her down. "One of those two."

"You didn't happen to catch a license plate number or the model of car," I said.

"No."

I didn't expect that she had, but that was okay. I had a hunch, and if it was right, I thought I knew how I could find the car.

CHAPTER FORTY-NINE

I sat in the Charger while the air-conditioning fought the heat that had built up in the car in the few minutes since I had shut it off. I rummaged in the armrest compartment and found the business card for the only insurance agent in town, and punched the number into my cell phone.

When Jerry Douglas came on the line I identified myself and was told to hold on. The phone clunked in my ear, probably the handset being dropped on the desk, and a second later I heard the sound of a door closing. Douglas was back another second later.

"What can I do for you?" he said in a hushed voice.

"I'm wondering if The Captain has access to a body shop," I said.

"Why?"

"You don't want to know."

"You're right, I don't."

"But does he?" I said.

"Yes," Douglas said. "He owns Schmidt's Auto Body out on the west side of town, right on Michigan Ave. We send all of our customers there who have claims."

That was exactly what I wanted to hear. "Do you know if you have sent a green, or maybe blue, sedan there recently? Possibly with front end damage?"

Douglas told me to hold on again, and I heard a computer keyboard clicking and clacking. "Actually, we did. A blue Ford Fusion. The owner said he hit a deer."

"Who's the owner?"

"Cliff Johnson."

"Son of a bitch," I said. My hunch was right, but how was I going to prove anything? That seemed to be the central theme with this case. I knew a hell of a lot more than I could prove.

CHAPTER FIFTY

Schmidt's Auto Body was at the bottom of the hill that the catholic church sat atop. It was surrounded by one of those sheet metal fences, but from the parking lot of the church I could see over the fence and into the back lot of the body shop. There was a blue Ford with front end damage sitting in the lot protected from view from the road. Was that a coincidence?

I got Julie Runyon on the phone.

"I'll bet you a dollar I'm looking at the car that hit Officer Ford," I said.

"Is that right?"

"It is," I said. I then told her how I had come to be where I was, and why I thought it was the car. "We need to get a search warrant for that car. I can't tell for sure, but I think I can see blood on it."

"Okay," Julie said, "number one, the blood is probably from the deer that the owner said he hit."

"Do we really believe—"

"And second, I know you are a seasoned investigator, and your hunch might be right—"

"It is."

"—but no judge is going to give us a warrant based on your hunch."

"That's bullshit," I said.

"What can I say, Chase?" Julie said. "Judges are like that. Evidence. We need evidence."

I was angry and frustrated when I disconnected. Evidence. It was always about evidence with these lawyers. I sat and stewed for a few minutes, and then I saw an unmarked patrol car exiting the church parking lot from the driveway on the other side of the church. It was Michael Hannigan. Without really thinking about it, I dropped the Charger into drive and took up pursuit.

I followed the police chief down the hill from the church. We took a left onto Michigan Ave. and headed toward downtown. I wasn't trying to go unnoticed; I was right on his bumper. I didn't care if he knew I was there or not. We cruised through downtown and turned right when we hit the Dairy Queen. Twenty seconds later, Hannigan turned into the driveway of a two story condo sitting atop a two car garage.

I followed him right into the driveway as the garage door started up. The unmarked eased into the garage. I came to a halt, slammed the transmission into park and leapt from the car. The garage door was still up when Hannigan climbed from his car.

"Hey, asshole," I said a little too loud, marching toward the open garage.

The police chief was startled and went for his gun as he turned toward me.

"Don't do it," I said.

Hannigan recognized me and stopped. "What the hell are you doing?" he said. "Have you lost your mind?"

"Not yet," I said. I came to stop just under the garage door. This way the safety device wouldn't let it close in my face, but I wasn't actually in his home.

He took a calming breath and then said, "What do you want?"

"What do I want? I want to put you and your father and your psycho brother in jail."

"For what?"

"Kidnapping, extortion, murder, hit and run, assault on a police officer. I don't really care which, but I'd really like to get the murder."

"Whoa, wait a minute," he said, holding up his hands like he was directing traffic.

"I know your sister isn't your sister."

"What?"

"Your real sister died shortly after birth, and you and your father stole Randy Adams' baby to replace her."

"Now I know you've lost your mind," Hannigan said. "We did not steal a baby."

"Yeah, you did," I said. "I have a witness who saw you at Woodstock with the baby. I also spoke with the priest who made the switch. And, just for good measure, I have a DNA match that links Meredith to her real mother."

"You have—"

"The problem I have is, the statute of limitations ran out on kidnapping a long time ago. However, if we can prove that there has been an ongoing conspiracy to cover up the crime, we can probably put you away for it."

Hannigan was totally knocked out of whack. "Ongoing conspiracy?"

"Yeah," I said. "That would involve the murders of Randy Adams and Peter Wilson, and the attempted murder of Officer Ford. You might have been able to prove that the conspiracy ended with the murder of Peter Wilson, but when you ran down Ford, you continued it again."

"When I—"

"Yeah, you."

"I didn't—"

"I think you did. And the car you did it with is sitting behind your dad's body shop."

Michael Hannigan sighed. "I asked you to let this go," he said.

"Well, I didn't," I said.

"No, you didn't." He turned and disappeared through the door to his condo.

CHAPTER FIFTY-ONE

I drove back to the Dairy Queen to cool off, both mentally and physically. I also needed to try to think. I don't always think very well when I'm angry. I got a Boston Cooler from the DQ and sat in my car sipping it carefully. I didn't need a brain freeze at that point. I replayed the conversation with Michael Hannigan and realized I had told him of my suspicion that the Ford Fusion at Schmidt's Auto Body had been used to run down Ford. See what I mean about not thinking when I'm mad?

I pulled out of the DQ and headed back to the church. It was after six and the shop was closed, but I could still see activity inside the building. I was pretty sure that Michael Hannigan hadn't been driving the Fusion when it hit Ford, but his brother or Cliff Johnson probably had been and if Michael knew that, or thought he knew that, then there was a very good possibility that he would tip them off, and any evidence of the hit and run would be gone. I was going to have to watch the car until something happened that would give Julie Runyon probable cause to get a search warrant.

I finished the Boston Cooler and turned on the Tigers game on the radio. The Angels were in town and Verlander was facing Weaver. At least I'd have a good game to listen to while I sat staring at the car. By the end of the second neither team had managed to reach base. I was settling in for a good old fashioned pitchers' duel, when one of the overhead garage doors at Schmidt's Auto Body clattered up and a kid in a backward red baseball cap came trotting out. He went directly to the blue Fusion, climbed into it, and drove it through the open door. Then the door clattered shut. I held my breath for what seemed an hour, and then the kid in the red hat and a man in khakis exited through the pedestrian door next to the overhead door. They got into separate cars and drove away.

I wanted to run right down there, jump the fence, and see what was going on inside that building. But it wasn't even eight o'clock yet and in Michigan, in the summer, it doesn't get dark until almost ten. If I stormed the castle walls at that point I'd have zero cover. I didn't want to run down there with no cover, without knowledge of what was going on. I was dumb, but I wasn't that dumb. So, I spent the next two hours listening to one of the best baseball games of the year. However, I was so distracted by what, if anything, was going on inside that body shop that I don't even remember what the final score was.

The game ended and the sun finally went down. The night sky darkened and crickets started to sing their mating call. I climbed out of the Charger and stretched a little before heading down the hill. I jumped up and grabbed the top of the wall. My feet hit the wall and the sheet metal let out a crash that would have woke the dead. Somewhere in the distance a dog with a Barry White bark told me he didn't appreciate the noise I had made. I pulled myself up and peeked over the wall like Kilroy. While the darkness made it so that others couldn't see me, it also made it so that I couldn't see others. But I didn't see or hear anything, so I pulled myself up the rest of the way, slung my feet over the wall and dropped down on the other side.

I darted from car to car in a zig zag pattern, staying low and hopefully out of sight. I made it to the building and found a window through which I peeked into the shop. There were no lights on inside, which was both good and bad. Good because nobody was working on the Fusion, bad because I couldn't see a damn thing in there. I tested the window and was pleasantly surprised when it slid up. I was just about the climb through when a gun was pressed to the back of my head.

"Don't move, or I'll blow your brains out."

CHAPTER FIFTY-TWO

I sat in a small office in the corner of the body shop. A window looked out into the body shop. The good news was that I could see the Fusion. It didn't look like it had been touched yet. The bad news was that I was locked in the office and was being watched by an armed guard.

The armed guard was the kid in the red hat that I had seen leave earlier. Apparently he had doubled back at some point; probably when I kicked the fence and alerted the entire town to my actions. Up close the kid was no more than 18. He was skinny, as if made out of pipe cleaners, and fair skinned with lots of freckles. Reddish-brown hair peeked out from under the hat and seven or eight reddish-brown hairs sprouted from his chin. A black and tan rottweiler with a head the size of a hubcap roamed the interior of the shop. The dog outweighed the kid by twenty or thirty pounds. Every now and then the dog let out one of the Barry White barks. I supposed it was lucky the kid had stopped me before I got through the window. The dog probably would have eaten me.

I had been in the office fifteen or twenty minutes when the pedestrian door next to the overhead garage door opened, and Frank Hannigan walked in. He went directly to the kid and they spoke soft enough that I couldn't hear what they were saying. Then Frank put his arm around the kid and walked him to the door. The kid left and Frank closed the door behind him.

Frank then walked over to the office, a big smile on his face, and opened the door. "My grandson," he said. "Great kid." Then the smile left. "On your feet."

I stood and caught an uppercut in the gut. I hadn't been ready and I doubled over as my breath was expelled. It put me in the perfect position for the knee that came next. My face exploded with pain and blood burst from my nose. The force straightened me back up. Frank grabbed two fists full of my shirt, dragged me from the office and hurled me across the shop.

The dog was excited by the commotion. He barked and jumped around as if cheering on a UFC fight.

I caught myself and breathed heavily through my mouth, trying to get my lungs to re-inflate. Frank stalked toward me. He had the biggest wrench I had ever seen in my life clenched in his right hand. I waited for him to swing, and then spun away. The wrench missed and the momentum of the swing carried Frank past me. I took one step forward and dug a right hook into his kidney. The force drove him to a knee and I took the opportunity the kick him in the ribs. He went down the rest of the way and I lined up to finish him off with a field goal style kick to the head, just like the one I had received in the back room of The Captain's Den.

"Enough!"

I turned to see Michael Hannigan standing just inside the shop. He had a pistol pointed at us.

"Shut up, Fred," he said.

The dog stopped barking and lay down with his head on his paws. He looked disappointed that the fight had ended.

Michael walked across the shop floor and helped his brother up and into a chair. He then tossed me a shop rag. I put the rag to my face and felt the cartilage in my nose compress from the contact. Michael paced back and forth with his hands on his hips. He walked over to the blue Fusion and squatted to inspect the front end.

"Is this the car?"

I started to answer but Michael continued before I could.

"Is this the car, Frank?" he said. He stood up and walked back to his brother. "Is this the car you used to run down my officer?"

My mouth fell open. I looked back and forth between the two Hannigan brothers.

Frank sat with his elbows on his knees and his head in his hands. "Call Dad," he said.

"No, Frank. I'm not calling Dad. This is our mess and we're going to clean it up."

I didn't like the sound of that. I started to look around for something to use as a weapon.

Frank slowly brought his head up. A wry grin creased his face. "Now you're talking," he said. "How do you want to do it? Are you going to shoot him, or can I finish him off?"

"You finish him off? He was about to finish you off when I stopped him."

Frank started to stand, slowly. "I'm getting my second wind."

"Sit down, Frank," Michael said. "Nobody is finishing anybody off."

"But Dad wants—"

"I don't care what Dad wants."

Frank was speechless. I could see it on his face. I doubted that anyone ever said they didn't care what The Captain wanted.

"Dad wanted me to steal a baby, for God's sake" Michael said. "And Dad wanted you to kill Peter Wilson to cover it up. And now Dad had you run down Officer Ford to cover up the cover up. This has got to stop. I'm done. I'm turning myself in."

"You're what?"

"And you're coming with me."

"Like hell I am," Frank said. He charged his brother and hit him with a full body block. Michael was caught off guard. He flew backwards and landed with a thud on the concrete floor. The gun he had held slipped from his grip and slid across the floor. Frank scrambled after it, but not fast enough. I drilled him with the kick to the head that had been denied earlier. He went down hard, face first on the cement floor and didn't move.

EPILOGUE

Michael Hannigan turned himself in and agreed to testify against his brother and his father. Since his crime was 40 years old, and he didn't actually kill anybody, the prosecutor gave him immunity in exchange for his testimony. Michael also had to agree to "retire." I almost felt bad for him, having been "retired" myself.

True to his nature, Frank didn't going down without a fight. He lost the fight when a battalion of state police officers descended on Saline to get him. The prosecutor had Michael's testimony, my testimony, and the testimony of about half the town to use against Frank. Along with the physical evidence that was left on the Ford Fusion, Frank was going to spend the rest of his life in prison.

Unfortunately, The Captain passed away in his sleep before he could be brought to trial. The citizens of Saline were robbed of their day in court, but they all turned out for the funeral. I was told that it was the biggest funeral the town had ever seen. I doubt that it was out of respect for the man. I'd bet a dollar that they all showed up to make sure he was actually dead.

I wasn't at the funeral, but I was back in Saline a couple months later on a crisp, cool, perfect Michigan fall day. I picked Meredith up at her office and drove her to the evangelical home. She was nervous, but excited to learn something of her biological father's family. She had already gotten quite friendly with Caroline Wolf and her half-sister Sara. She had donated the bone marrow to Sara and it looked as if she was going to be okay, for now.

We entered the EVH through the airlock and immediately ran into Misti with an i. She smiled at me until she saw that I was with Meredith, and then she scowled. I said hi and kept moving. We found Mrs. Adams in her usual spot in the blue reception area.

"Hello, Mrs. Adams," I said. "Do you remember me?"

She studied me for a second, and then said, "Of course. You're the Miller boy from down the street. Lucy's son."

I smiled and didn't correct her. "I have someone I want you to meet," I said. I pulled Meredith to my side. "This is your granddaughter, Meredith."

The old lady smiled and a tear escaped the corner of her eye. "I knew you'd come," she said.

Author's Note

First, I know that American Coney Island does not serve breakfast. I wanted to get the Detroit landmark into the story and that's where it fit.

Next, Saline is a real town. It's my hometown, where I was raised and where I still live. I had to set the story somewhere and thought, "Why not Saline?" That said, none of the characters in the story are real. I was inspired by some real people and places, but it's all a figment of my imagination. If you think it's you, it's not. Please don't sue me.

Finally, I want to thank everyone who helped to get this story published. If I try to name everybody I'm sure I will miss some, so I won't try.

Thank you very much for reading. I hope you enjoyed it.

Steve